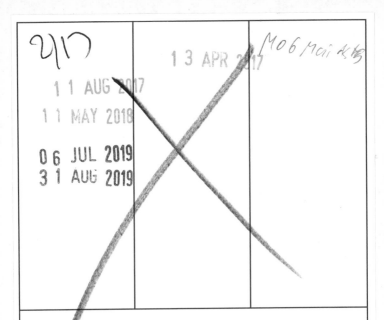

Books should be returned or renewed by the last
date above. Renew by phone **03000 41 31 31** or
online *www.kent.gov.uk/libs*

D1424972

DEAD MAN RIVER

At first, it seemed to Dave Brent like a wonderful solution to his troubles: exchange identities with the dead man he found floating in the river, and that should be the last he'd hear of the Vandemanns, who wanted his blood. But the dead man was more popular than Dave reckoned — and a lot of men want to find the one now using his name. If they catch him, they intend to offer him a choice of deaths — by torture or a quick bullet. Dave isn't keen on either option . . .

TYLER HATCH

◆

DEAD MAN RIVER

Complete and Unabridged

LINFORD
Leicester

First published in Great Britain in 2015 by
Robert Hale Limited
London

First Linford Edition
published 2017
by arrangement with
Robert Hale
an imprint of The Crowood Press
Wiltshire

A catalogue record for this book is available
from the British Library.

ISBN 978–1–4448–3165–8

Published by
F. A. Thorpe (Publishing)
Anstey, Leicestershire

Set by Words & Graphics Ltd.
Anstey, Leicestershire
Printed and bound in Great Britain by
T. J. International Ltd., Padstow, Cornwall

This book is printed on acid-free paper

1

The River

It was more than likely the results of the third bushwhacker's head shot that threw Dave Brent off his usual quick thinking — and almost cost him his life.

But that part came later, a couple of weeks after he was ambushed when he least expected it. The shot came as he rode through a draw that damn half-breed had assured him hadn't been used for months and led to safe country — assured him for almost the last of his money and a handful of rifle cartridges. *Sucker, serves you right!*

His black mount was uneasy but Dave thought it was because the draw was narrow, the walls giving a feeling of being about to topple down.

It was lucky they made him leery: when seeking a way to calm the mount

1

he looked up at the ragged walls just in time to see the fading sunlight flash along the angled barrel of a rifle. He didn't hesitate, threw himself out of the saddle, taking his own rifle with him. He twisted wildly, not hearing the shot from above, but seeing dirt and stone erupt just below where he would fall. Later, he couldn't remember how he did it, but he managed to hit on his left side and somehow propelled himself behind a rock. The next two shots snarled off it, spouting grit. A bullet already in the breech, Dave wrenched the rifle around, spotted the shooter half-rising to lever in his next shell. Dave and the killer fired simultaneously and suddenly the world was a red place, then a pulsing black as lightning seared through his skull. He was knocked flat but didn't pass out completely.

He lay there, actually paralysed for a few seconds, but aware enough to see the bushwhacker toppling down the slope, starting a small avalanche.

Then the blackness spread with a

falling sensation and he didn't feel his face strike the ground . . .

⋆ ⋆ ⋆

It was agonizing to wake up, head pounding like he had been kicked by a horse, teeth aching from the jar, half-blinded in the left eye by sticky, coagulating blood. He was surprised to see his mount calmly chomping away at some grass a few yards away.

'You — sonuver — *gun*!' he gritted, yet with a fondness he wasn't aware of feeling earlier. He crawled across and the animal merely stared at him as its jaws worked.

Afterwards he figured the horse had stood still while he dragged himself up to the dangling saddle canteen and fell back clutching it.

He had no idea how long it took him to slake his raging thirst, wash his eyes free of blood, soak his neckerchief and hold it in place over the shallow head-wound by jamming down his hat,

3

cocked at a precarious angle.

The sun was barely a spark above the distant peaks when he found the bushwhacker. To his surprise the man was still alive — barely. Dave gave him water and looked at the oozing chest wound.

'Not too good, *amigo*.'

The man nodded vaguely, made a growling noise.

'Why you tryin' to kill me?' Dave asked. 'I dunno you.'

After several attempts the bushwhacker managed to grate, 'Bounty . . . '

'There's no bounty on me, mister!' Dave said, outraged. 'You got the wrong man. I'm no outlaw.'

The man grabbed his arm, weakly, his blood-flecked lips working until finally he managed to rasp: 'Van . . . V-v . . . Vande — '

Dave went rigid. 'Christ! So that's how they figure to nail me!' He shook his head slowly. 'And I thought I'd shaken 'em weeks ago!'

He ought to have known better,

realized those other two times men had jumped him during the past few weeks were not just desperadoes looking for easy pickings, but making their try at a goddamn *bounty* put on him by Will Vandemann.

By God! I'd better quit thinkin' like a schoolgirl and start acting like the thirty-five-year-old hardcase I'm s'posed to be, if I aim to see year thirty-six . . .

It was a painful pill to swallow, but he had to admit he had badly underestimated the Vandemanns.

The sons of bitches were never going to give up until they'd seen him *dead!*

A week later — a week of doubling back on his trail, going over almost unclimbable mountains instead of taking the easier route around the base, a week of sleeping away from his camp-fire, his blankets humped up to make it look as if he was in his bedroll — instead, shivering behind some boulder or bush, hands cold-cramped from holding his rifle at the ready.

He still had headaches and slight vision disturbances, but got a good way north in that time without further trouble and was now feeling a hell of a lot more confident of making it all the way to his destination.

The river he reached was about as wild as he'd ever seen, but working south for a time, he suddenly came to a broad, shallow stretch; the water as clear as ice.

He decided without hesitation that here was where he would make his crossing: it was the best place to ford he'd come across in seven days' hard riding.

By now, he ought to be free of pursuit by the Vandemanns, but that Big Will was totally unforgiving and if they were still coming, they would figure here was one of the places where he would choose to cross.

But he had to get to the other side and find the trail to Bixby; he was afraid he might have already come too far and missed it. The only way to find out for sure was to cross *here* and with luck he could be well along the Southern Run Trail by dark.

The big black, with the star-blaze on its chest and a very white tip on the left ear, had cost him a deal of time and sweat — not to mention money — and they were still trying to get used to each other, but he felt there was a good rapport developing.

So he helped the horse pick its way carefully into the stream and allowed it to stop to drink, cool water almost lapping its belly. While it drank he hooked a leg over the saddlehorn and began to build a cigarette from his dwindling supply of tobacco. Licking the paper, he noticed the water surging a little around the black's legs and took this as a sign of a stronger current towards midstream.

The horse was ready to slurp up a few gallons of the clear water after the long slog over some of the roughest country Dave Brent had encountered in a coon's age, but he decided to curb the horse's enthusiasm when he got his cigarette alight.

It was when he exhaled the first satisfying deep-down draw of smoke that he froze, while shaking out the vesta.

There was a dead man caught up by a half-submerged deadfall in a quiet backwater. He *had* to be dead, face down, an arm hooked in a broken branch of the waterlogged tree, clothes tattered, part of his vest and shirt ripped off, exposing white flesh with jagged rock cuts, the blood long washed away.

Closer inspection showed this man must have come from high upriver, likely slammed onto the jagged rocks of rapids he recalled, foaming and roaring like a hundred small waterfalls, then drifted in here to quieter waters out of the mainstream.

'*Damn!*' he said aloud. He didn't fancy riding into Bixby with a dead man across his saddle but — well, he couldn't leave the poor devil here for the wild animals, either.

It wasn't a pleasant job going through the corpse's pockets and he did it with breath hissing between his teeth, trying to avoid the torn-up flesh from the dead man's rough passage before he washed in here.

He found a buckskin wallet wrapped in a square of oilskin, held tightly closed by several turns of a rawhide thong. He stripped this away with some difficulty, it being so tight, no doubt to protect the wallet's contents from the water. There were traces of original Indian beading on the flap. Inside the wallet he found a couple of papers but no money.

The thickest paper, folded several times, was an Army Discharge — *Dishonourable* Discharge — from the Fifth Cavalry while stationed at Fort McCook, Nebraska.

It was issued for having struck an officer.

'Now why in hell would anyone want to keep something like that!' Dave wondered half aloud.

The writing was barely legible, some water obviously having found its way past the oilskin. As far as Dave could make out, the name was *Walter Patrick Craig*, aged 35 years at the time — about three years ago, he saw by the date beside the name of the officer who had signed the papers.

And Walt Craig had been a bad soldier, it seemed: twice promoted to corporal and both times reduced to private within weeks for fighting — '*and otherwise bringing disrepute to himself and his company, which reflected adversely upon the United States Army in general . . .* '

'Seems you won't be greatly missed, Walt.' Then, as he started to push the papers back into the damp wallet, Dave Brent paused. He felt his heart give a jump or two.

'Mebbe — just *mebbe* — I can make use of your shortcomings, Walt, in exchange for my own!'

Those crazy, vengeful Vandemann brothers were still somewhere along his

10

backtrail and here might be as good a place as any to set things up and hopefully end their relentless pursuit.

As the thoughts began to form now — at an alarming rate, too! — he looked more critically at the body: yeah, Mr Walter P. Craig, deceased, was about the same size as Dave Brent — perhaps Dave had an inch or two extra in height — but the general body-size would fit well enough. The hair — it was blacker than Dave's, but he could get by with his dark-brown locks. The face — well, there was no face. Poor Walt had obviously been washed the full length of those awful rapids and even his own mother wouldn't recognize him. Dave could leave his own four-day stubble on, anyway, for a while, until he got used to his new identity.

All he had to do was take Walt Craig's papers and leave a couple bearing his own name: the bill of sale for the big black, from Trumbo Flats, way, way south of here, a receipt from a gunsmith in Yellow Sky for replacing the shattered firing pin in his Winchester, his almost empty tobacco sack with the name of the store where he had bought it in Trumbo Flats at the same time as he got the black mount on the label tag, an old letter from his half-brother, Luke, who had later drowned while helping a bunch of greenhorn settlers across a flooded river. *He had kept the letter long enough and Luke was long gone.*

That would be enough. He had only a couple of dollars in cash and some change and reluctantly shoved in two dimes and, after a long hesitation, his only half-dollar coin . . .

He stood back, breathing quite hard, idly rubbing the slowly healing bullet burn across his left temple, which throbbed dully, and scratched at his tousled hair.

'Well, Dave Brent — here you lie — for better or for worse!'

He glanced at the Army Discharge once again and smiled slowly. 'And welcome to beautiful Wyoming, Yew-nited States of Ay-merica, Mr Walter P. Craig. May those Vandemann bastards never lay eyes on you!'

So Dave Brent started out across this tributary of the Green River, but Walter P. Craig rode the black gelding across to the other side . . .

* * *

The dead man, carrying Dave's papers now, rocked languidly, and the slow-moving water nudged at his ragged and torn boots, swung his legs into the sluggish current, which tugged him slowly round a bend with gradually increasing speed, downstream.

Damn current's strengthening a little, Dave thought in mild alarm, as he climbed aboard his mount, noticed the tip of the right ear was showing palely now — he would have to rub some more charcoal from his next camp-fire into it — and check the white star-blaze on the muscled chest.

Best to keep those blazes covered for a spell, he decided, settling into leather and urging the big horse forward.

As he rode along the river-bank, watching the corpse drift leisurely downstream, he suddenly hauled rein and there was a strange, very brief fluttering in his belly.

'Judas Priest!' he breathed. 'Wh-what the hell am I *doing*?'

He must be crazy! As he had the thought, he rubbed again at the dull, throbbing ache in his temple, edged by the bullet burn. His head was throbbing but he wasn't sure if it had started the moment he realized the stupid mistake he'd made or whether it had been there all along and he had been too busy to notice.

Well, *hell*! He was glad he *did* notice it before it got any worse and blanked him out on what he had done!

It was simple, really: he had left the receipt for the black horse with the real Walter Craig. That was fine, it would help convince whoever was looking that he had found Dave Brent — *except he, now as Walt Craig, was riding the same damned horse described in the bill of sale.*

If some lawman was involved, and he would be whenever the body was found, he would want to know what Dave was doing riding the mount described on that receipt . . . in someone else's name.

He could even be accused of stealing the horse from the dead man and — There was no way it would fool the Vandemanns, not one tiny bit!

'Aaah! This damn headache!' Then he decided the hell with what had made him act so slipshod, he had better get on with putting the matter right.

He hipped in the saddle, looking for the body, wondering where it had lodged this time . . .

To his horror, he couldn't see it along the bank where he had expected it to catch in the brush which grew right down to the water's edge.

No! There was a drop at the end of

this large pool and Craig had drifted in with the increased tug caused by the river gathering speed as it approached that drop.

He was moving as his aching head figured what had happened: there was a small waterfall at the drop, increasing the drag, strengthening the normal current. And, as Dave watched helplessly, the dead man's legs swung into that current, projected out over the edge for a moment — then the body swiftly dropped out of sight.

As Walter P. Craig disappeared, he heard excited shouts from someone below as they watched Craig's body plunging down towards them.

2

The Legend

Dave loosened the Colt in its holster instinctively, fought the suddenly skittish black, which no doubt was alarmed by the increasing pressure of the water on its legs and rolling-eyed glimpses of the river way below the drop-off.

Standing in the stirrups at one stage, Dave glimpsed a little drama below, about a dozen feet down.

The body had been whisked over the ledge and had plummeted into a shallow pool where three tousled-haired boys had apparently been fishing, but, now, were standing rigidly in water that came to their knees, staring at the body that had apparently dropped out of the sky.

There was a redhead, one with black, curly hair, and the third had short-cropped pale-blond hair.

It was this one who looked up and saw Dave sitting his horse almost at the very edge of the drop-off.

'H-hey, mister!' the piping voice called above the sound of the small waterfall. 'Is this . . . yours?'

He pointed to Craig's body and started to back off as one of Craig's arms drifted in and brushed his leg. He dropped his fishing pole and clawed at the bank, the other two boys quickly following. The redhead stood up, dropping his pole now, and said, 'I'm gonna fetch Uncle Lew! He's just upstream.'

'Hey, Red!' shouted the one with black curly hair. 'Don't forget he told us not to come up near this waterfall!'

'I-I'm gonna fetch him anyway!'

The redhead started running along the bank and was soon out of sight around a bend. The other two stood staring up at Dave, who was putting his horse down a narrow trail now. The two boys looked at each other uncertainly.

'Maybe we shoulda gone with him!'

18

the blond one said, watching Dave warily.

Dave was riding in slowly by then: he had no choice: the kids had seen him and could easily describe him. He had it in mind to tell them some story while appearing to be innocent of knowledge of the dead man now nudging a small projection of the bank, the legs moving slightly with the push of the current . . . but he didn't know just what to say.

The boys stayed close, watching every step the big black took in their direction. Then the curly-haired one suddenly grinned.

'Here comes Red! He said his uncle was settin' his fish traps this mornin', just over the rise.'

Dave heaved a sigh as he saw the red-haired boy come racing over a small rise, hair blowing, followed by a long-striding tall man with red hair that matched the kid's protruding from under his hat. Then Dave's smile faded.

He held a rifle in one hand and, when he saw Dave, slowed, levered, and jerked the barrel slightly.

'What we got here?' he asked in a deep voice, loud enough to be heard easily over the noise of the waterfall; it sounded like a voice used to getting answers to questions asked and Dave's insides tightened: *surely he hadn't had the ill luck to run into a damn lawman so soon!*

The panting kid was clinging to his uncle's trousers on the left side now.

The curly-haired boy pointed at Dave. 'He was on top of the falls, Mr Burns! We think he dumped — that — but din' know we was here.'

'And fishin' close to the falls where I told you not to!' snapped Burns, but he gave most of his attention to Dave. 'You wanna climb down, mister?'

Dave didn't move, saw the man tense, but relax again as Dave folded his hands on the saddlehorn. 'I can talk just as well from here.'

'Long as you only talk. Who's the dead'un?'

Dave shook his head, pointing

behind. 'Seen him floating up there, but the current caught him and dropped him over the falls before I had a chance to get to him.'

Burns kept his face blank as he stared levelly at Dave. 'Well, you just stay put while *I* take a look — I mean it! Stay put!'

Dave obeyed and watched with gritted teeth while the red-haired man gingerly opened the dead man's soggy clothes and reached into his pockets. 'Who're you, by the way?'

'Just a drifter heading for Bixby.'

'I meant your name!'

'Don't see that it matters, but it's Walt Craig. What's yours?'

Burns blinked, frowned and said, slowly, 'Lew Burns,' as he walked towards the body, stepped into knee-deep water, and used the rifle barrel to poke it hard enough to roll it over.

The blond boy was sick when the ugly, raw meat of the dead face appeared. One of the others made a gagging sound and Burns grimaced.

'The hell done that to him?'

He lifted the rifle a little, pointing it at Dave's chest.

'Not me!' Dave said quickly. 'Like that when I found him. My guess is he fell in the river upstream. There's a whole slew of rapids up there and one of 'em runs through jagged rocks.'

'Yeah, I know it. That's why I always make sure Young Red and his pards do their fishin' down here. You boys wade ashore now and set some water boilin' for coffee.'

'Aw, Unk!' whined the small redhead. 'Can't we — ?'

'No you can't! You do what I told you — all of you!'

The boys wandered off and began to build a small camp-fire, the red-haired boy filling a coffee pot with water from the river — well above where the body was.

Dave helped Burns 'discover' the oilskin-wrapped wallet and Burns opened it with his work-hardened hands, swearing a little at the difficulty of the small chore. He quickly scanned the contents.

'Here's a bill of sale for a hoss, feller by the name of Dave Brent, it seems,' he said, waving some of the papers Dave had planted earlier. He read and reread them and twice Dave saw him glancing at the big black gelding munching on grass along the river-bank.

Dave tensed but Burns said nothing, folded the papers and put them in his pocket. With a small grunt he levered himself up with the help of his rifle. Suddenly, the weapon was pointing at Dave, startling him a little at the man's abrupt move.

'We'd best take the body into Bixby — it ain't far — and you, friend, better come along and tell your story to Sheriff Case Barlow.'

Dave frowned. 'Case Barlow? Is he still kicking?'

'Bixby's pride an' joy havin' a man like him as permanent lawman. Where you been, feller? Figured the whole blame country knew that.'

'Been way down south — workin' the Border spreads.'

Burns's eyes narrowed. 'That's range war territory, ain't it? Guns-for-hire, an' all that stuff.'

'Not any more. There's law moved in.'

Dave held the man's curious gaze steadily. *There was something about the way he looked — not just like a man who baited fish traps for leisure or necessity, but someone who knew his way around and analyzed everything that was said to him.*

His eyes swept once more over the way Dave carried his gun in a cutaway holster, with a neat notch removed at a level so his finger could find the trigger unerringly, the holster base tied down, not too low — nor too high.

Worn the way of a man who knew how to use a gun — quickly and confidently.

But Burns said no more, though Dave noticed his hands had tightened their grip on the rifle. Then Lew Burns cleared his throat and said quietly, 'Yeah, I think we better go see Sheriff Barlow.'

'Well, you're holding the gun.' Dave's voice was a mite tighter than he would have liked, but —

Burns nodded. 'I am. So, I figure it'd be best. Wouldn't want any of these boys mixed up in anythin'.'

'Relax, Burns, I've got no hassle with the law.'

'Not up here anyway, huh?'

Dave sighed. 'Now, why not leave things the way they are? No need to push and mebbe upset the apple cart.'

Burns licked his lips, glanced at the boys who were standing watching the two men now, sensing the sudden tension but not sure what it was all about.

'Yeah, well, we wouldn't wanna do that, would we? It's that hoss of yours that bothers me, Craig. I can see it's got a couple of blaze marks, on the chest and one ear, but they look — I dunno

— kinda only half-showin', like you might've tried to cover 'em up an' the water's partly washed 'em off.'

'Why would I want to do that?'

'Well, I'm Case Barlow's deputy and I kinda pick up on these things. See, if them marks *are* there and've been covered up, well, that horse would fit the description on that bill of sale Brent's carryin' — with his name on it.'

'Well, why don't we go see Case Barlow and sort things out?'

Burns nodded carefully. 'Glad you think it's a good idea . . . '

The implication being that it really wouldn't have mattered even if Dave hadn't figured it that way. *And he didn't!*

He felt mighty uneasy with a legendary man like Case Barlow being brought into this: he had the name for being mighty tough. Some said he made his own law, or twisted it to suit.

If it hadn't been for those wide-eyed boys, Dave may have given Burns an argument, but, they *were* here, so that was that. No gunplay — at least none that would be started by the new Walter P. Craig.

'Well, let's get it done. How far's Bixby?'

'We'll be there before sundown.'

Maybe Dave could have hoped they would arrive after dark just in case he had to make a run for it but, at the same time, this was a chance to find out for sure if his switch of identities was going to work.

If it didn't — well, he had no illusions: he could never match the gunspeed of a man like Case Barlow — even if the sheriff was in his sixties.

* * *

Dave was surprised.

He had heard hundreds of stories about Case Barlow over the years, but this was the first time he had set eyes on the man.

Maybe because of the daring deeds Barlow was said to have done over the years, Dave had always pictured the legendary lawman as a man who rode tall in the saddle. But Barlow was not only short — no more than five feet six in his high-heeled boots — he was slim and slightly bent in the middle, and may have given a small wince of pain as he shuffled his feet and set them more firmly on the old piece of carpet under his desk chair. He looked his age — just another old man with rheumatics, plus a wheeze and a cough, likely from his trademark cheroots, reportedly made specially for him in Caracas, Venezuela from tobacco that would choke a mountain lion.

His eyes were rheumy, almost dreamy, as Burns handled the introductions. Case Barlow didn't offer to shake hands, but Dave figured he would know how much change he had in his hip pocket.

'Who we got here, Lew?'

'Calls himself Walter P. Craig, Case. There's another feller roped across the saddle out back. Craig says he found him floatin' in the river — but he can tell you himself.' *Was there a kind of doubt in Burns's tone, as if he was quietly alerting Barlow to something?*

But Dave had the floor whether he wanted it or not and he gave a brief description of how he had found the real Walter P. Craig — only he made sure he identified him as 'Dave Brent'.

Case Barlow surprised Dave by offering him a cheroot, which he took and lit up, coughing, despite efforts not to.

'Good tobacco,' he croaked, and there may have been just a smidgen of a smile on Barlow's thin lips. He had a kind of puckered face, not too mean, and sure not too friendly — somewhere in between — at least until the man had made up his mind about the situation.

'Too bad Brent's corpse got away from me. Hope it didn't scare them boys too much, Burns.'

'Give 'em plenty to tell their schoolmates when vacation's over. They'll all be heroes!'

Dave smiled and even Case Barlow gave a brief chuckle. He hadn't taken his eyes off Dave and now asked, 'You got some identification, Mr Craig?'

'Yeah, I guess.' Dave fumbled in his pockets and brought out the Army Discharge, handed it to Barlow, who took his time reading it, then gave Dave that steady, disturbing stare.

'Funny thing for a man to carry about with him. Hardly flattering.'

Dave shrugged, trying to look a mite sheepish. 'Yeah, lot of folk say that, but — well, I was a bit younger and a lot more foolish in those days, but finally come to my senses. So I decided to keep the discharge. I-I feel sort of a twinge of shame each time I read it, but it reminds me not to act so damn foolish again.'

Barlow made no comment, opened a desk drawer and took out a thick, untidy bundle of handbills. Dave felt a sudden prickle of sweat under his arms as the sheriff began checking the bills without comment.

'You won't find me on any dodgers, Sheriff,' Dave said, trying to sound casual.

Barlow went on flicking through the handbills. Then suddenly he paused and Dave's belly tightened: *Judas!* Surely there wasn't one with Walt Craig's name on it!

But Barlow merely continued working his way through the pile. Dave's heart was hammering so hard he thought the lawman must hear it. Then the sheriff stopped riffling the bills and stared long and expressionlessly at Dave, who was damned if he was going to say another word — unless asked.

'Well . . . ' the sheriff said finally, 'nothin' here, but I watched you and Lew ride up to my hitchrail' — he gestured to a pair of battered field-glasses resting on a wooden tray almost overflowing with papers, both hand-written and printed — 'and I gotta tell you that black hoss you're forkin' is mighty close to the description of the one in that bill of sale Brent's carryin'.

Blazes're not very clear, either faded, dirty or mebbe even deliberately blotted out . . . You got somethin' to say, son?'

Dave reached a sudden decision: he knew that of all the people in this world, the most dangerous one he could meet in his present situation was standing not three feet from him *and he was no man to tangle with!*

'All right,' he said heavily. 'It is the same horse. I figured Brent wouldn't be needing it, and it followed me around and nuzzled me — '

'So you reckoned that entitled you to keep the hoss for yourself?' the lawman said flatly.

Dave hesitated, then nodded curtly. 'My own mount had brought me a long way and I figured it was about time he had some freedom so I transferred the saddle to the black and turned my mount loose.'

'What was he like, this one you set free?'

Damn! He might've known a man like Barlow would want all the details.

'Aw, nothin' special, just another workin' sorrel.'

'Like every second or third hoss in this neck of the woods,' Burns added, and Barlow nodded agreement.

'Guess most men would've done the same as you, son, but it ain't somethin' I'd encourage. You'd've been better not leavin' that bill of sale describin' the black so well.'

Dave knew that now! But he didn't trust himself to speak. There was likely more to come: it was Dave Brent's name on that receipt.

'Well, we might get back to that. Meanwhile, there's another couple things I think we better iron out an' right now.' Barlow took his time screwing out his smoked-down cheroot in the coffee-can lid he used as an ashtray, not taking his chill gaze off Dave.

'What's that, Sheriff?' Dave asked, trying to appear a lot more relaxed than he felt.

A fly buzzed loudly for a long moment in the stuffy office, then Case

Barlow said, 'I knowed a Walter Patrick Craig some years back — and he didn't look a helluva lot like you, friend. Was wonderin' if you got anythin' to say about that?'

'Hell, Case, he *ain't* Walt Craig!' cut in Lew Burns as if right on cue! 'That bill of sale for the horse is in the name of Dave Brent an' there's a letter addressed to the same name. Seems to me that this feller could've switched identities, put papers in his name on the dead feller, then aimed to use Craig's name!'

'Now, I wonder why he'd go and do that?'

Dave glared at them both. 'You sound like a stage act! All *right*, dammit! I found Craig floatin', dead, just like I said and — and I've got some fellers on my tail who'll be right happy to see *me* dead. I — er — just figured if a dead man in Craig's condition turned up, carrying papers in my name, well, word would likely get back to the Vandemanns sometime, then mebbe

34

they'd reckon it was me and give up houndin' me.'

The old lawman continued to stare, face deadpan, and Burns looked at him, obviously waiting to see which way Barlow was going to jump.

Case Barlow was busy summing up the situation.

His features gave nothing away and although his gaze was turned in Dave's direction, the sweating cowboy had the impression he wasn't really being given the hard treatment — Barlow just happened to be looking that way while he thought things over.

Something to remember, though: Barlow was feeling his age! He needed time to make his decisions. That knowledge might just come in handy sometime: no longer the man of hair-trigger action that had made his reputation.

'Reckon I'd need more to go on than what I've got, son, but I tell you now, you could be lookin' at doin' some jail-time.'

Dave stiffened: old and unbending or not, Barlow meant what he said: jail-time. *Hell!*

'Look, Sheriff, it was a snap decision. I don't see that I've done anything wrong!'

'You don't, huh? Well, I'm here to tell you you're wrong there, *amigo*. Just because a man's dead, don't mean you can take his belongings. Sure, you can say he'd have no more use for 'em, and you'd be right, but he's bound to have kinfolk somewhere and *they* have first claim. So, takin' a man's hoss like that is just plain stealin' and that means jail-time in my book.'

Dave stared back coldly. 'You're a disappointment to me, Barlow. I figured all them things they say about you've got some roots in the truth, but right now you sound just like a petty old man to me.'

Burns sucked down a quick, audible breath, slowly shook his head. He didn't have to say anything.

Dave had already said too much.

3

Long ago — Far away

'Sheriff, are you willing to listen to my side of things?'

'Well, son, I'd be downright . . . *petty* . . . if I said no, wouldn't I?' Barlow quickly held up a hand as Dave started to speak. 'You go right ahead, I'll listen to what you have to say, and I'll be the one to make any decision that might be needed. That all right with you?'

Dave felt mighty uneasy: he sure didn't like the look in Barlow's eyes now. But he was pleased that his voice was steady, his words clear, when he answered.

'Suits me, Sheriff — er — I have to go back a'ways.'

'Take your time,' the lawman said firmly. 'No one's goin' anywhere right now.'

Dave winced inwardly: the lawman's choice of words might have been better! But he cleared his throat and started to tell his story . . .

★   ★   ★

'It was about eight months ago,' he began, 'a long way south of here — '

'Like down along the Border?' Lew Burns asked sharply, and Dave had an urge to smack the man in the mouth, seeing how Case Barlow's narrow shoulders tensed up some at the question. *Burns was turning out to be a man who enjoyed stirring up trouble. Something else to remember!*

'Yeah, as a matter of fact. Eight months ago, the Border troubles were winding down, but there was still a heap of *gringos* arriving, looking for a fast buck, and not much caring how they made it.'

'We need this background?' asked Burns impatiently, but before Dave could answer, Barlow said, tersely,

'Settin' a background never hurt none, Lew.' He flicked his eyes towards Dave. 'Just keep it brief, son.'

With a final glare at Burns, Dave continued.

'I was working the Border spreads at that time, as a bronc-buster but looking for more excitement, I guess. So I just quit one day and joined up with a bunch under a crazy Mex who called himself Diablo Rey, King of the Devils. Loco as they come but a pretty good man in a fight, planned his moves, not like most of them Border raiders who just charged in with machetes swinging and guns blazing at anything that moved . . . and we were well paid.'

'Mercenaries!' growled Burns.

'I've heard of that Mex!' Barlow said slowly, thoughtfully. His narrowed gave was cold as he set it on Dave. 'Like Lew says, you were one of them mercenaries?'

Dave shrugged. 'Told you, I was looking for excitement, had had a bellyful of ranch work and I needed some money, fast. I wasn't too keen on what I found so figured to make this my last raid. Thought I'd quit and come back to the States.'

Dave waited, thinking the man would have something to say to that, but when he didn't speak, continued, 'Well, trouble was Rey didn't just keep his raids below the Border agin the *rebeldes* we were being paid to wipe out: he liked to slip across the Rio from time to time and hit some of the big *Americano* spreads when they least expected it . . . blaming the rebs, of course. He'd take horses already broke to the saddle, cows used to being herded: made the getaway a lot easier.'

Case Barlow, mouth tight, nodded, and suddenly said, 'That's the son of a bitch who wiped out my wife's brother's ranch, burned it, then killed him and his family!'

He paused to clear his throat and knock the suggestion of a quavery edge off his voice. He signed with a jerky movement of his hand for Dave to continue. 'You got my full attention now, son.'

Dave wasn't sure whether that was a good thing or not.

A shortage of horses was never much of a problem, for Rey. There were two large *Americano* spreads close to the Border crossing so, crazy as a loon with home-brewed mescal, he ordered that both ranches be raided and so give them a bigger choice of good mounts.

In a single night, Rey's men came surging back across the Rio with at least fifty strong horses, all saddle broke, and used to the wild and rugged country, leaving behind a thick pall of gunsmoke, mixed with that of burning buildings . . . and some human flesh.

There had to be a celebration after such a success, of course, and the vino and tequila flowed freely. Dave decided to definitely make this his last time with Rey. Naturally, there were fights — mostly with guns and knives — and, once, a gory contest with naked machetes.

But while even more booze was being broken out, posses from the Yankee spreads — the Broken K and the Lazy V — swept in out of the night.

No quarter was asked, expected, or given.

It was swift and bloody work and Diablo Rey went to meet his namesake along with seventeen others of his men.

The *gringos* decided this called for a real wingding and, with a free supply of liquor readily available — raw and deadly though it was — *they* made a memorable *carouse*.

The fights were less violent but still bloody, and when they began to bore, someone said now that the Broken K had no legal owners left alive — which meant no fighting pay, or pay of any kind — why didn't they help themselves to some of these horses and steers the Mexes had so kindly rounded up for them?

Dave cheered with the rest, mingling

with the Border cowmen now. Earlier, his stomach had rebelled against the fiery chilli dishes the Mexican women had prepared. So he had not done as much indiscriminate drinking as the others, which kept his head quite a bit clearer. This made him more discerning in his selection of his 'prize' for winning a gruelling race that had killed a horse and seen two men end up with broken limbs.

He had noticed a big black earlier: it had a white tip on its left ear and a white blaze mark on its chest.

But he soon discovered he was not alone in admiring this animal's sleek lines and handsome bearing . . .

There were two men who gave him an argument when he tried to stake his claim. Fists flew, broken bottles appeared and, finally, someone went for his gun.

He was a cocky young *gringo* who couldn't hold his drink but his intentions were deadly serious as he pulled his Colt, steadied it in both hands and fired at Dave. The slug took Dave's hat off and his own gun came up blazing.

The young *gringo* went down without a sound, his boots leaving the ground before he landed flat on his back.

Dave swore. His reaction had been instinctive. *Dammit! He didn't want gunplay!*

Now the youngster's sidekick jumped in, swinging a machete, and Dave ducked under the whistling blade and came up inside the swinging arm and smashed the side of his still smoking Colt into the man's face. He stepped back as his assailant crumpled and another ranny, bending over the youngster Dave had shot, straightened, his face pale and tight in the firelight as he looked at Dave.

'Judas, Dave! You — you've killed young Harry Vandemann!'

The words cut through the noisy sounds of carousal and Dave tensed as he heard the growling, animal-like sounds of Big Will Vandemann — six feet six, and 200 pounds, mean as a grizzly with a bellyache. Spittle flew as he roared:

'You're dead, Brent! *D-e-d!* You hear me?'

His voice matched his massive chest, thundering through the camp, but, as he slapped a hand to his gun butt he paused, looking down the barrel of Dave's six-gun.

'He was trying to kill me,' Dave said flatly. 'You want to make *your* try, Will, why, you go right ahead!'

Slowly, the celebrations died down and men shuffled this way and that so that Dave found himself alone facing the three surviving Vandemann brothers: Will, and his two younger siblings, Pierce and Riley, the latter two looking to the big man for a lead, but somehow not seeming too enthusiastic, unable to take their eyes off Dave's cocked gun.

'You gents got any preferences here? Who tries first, I mean?' The gun moved in short, menacing arcs. 'How about you, Pierce? You're a cocky sonuver, always twirling your gun around your trigger finger. No? Aw, Riley, I've seen you shoot so I ain't gonna worry about you. Which brings us to you, Big Will. You gonna push this? Everyone here saw Harry coming at me . . . I had no choice.'

Big Will's jaws were clamped, knotted tension showing as he glared at Dave Brent. 'You killed him, Brent, so you — are — *dead*! Ah, you might have the drop now, but you won't live long. An' you — won't — die — fast! It'll be a *loooong* time before you finally croak! No one spills Vandemann blood and gets away with it!' Suddenly he roared at his two brothers, 'Grab him! *Now!*'

Pierce and Riley closed in on Dave without hesitation but he stood there, unmoving, gun held so he could shoot either one stupid enough to obey Big Will.

The brothers stopped, Pierce licking his lips, Riley glancing a mite shakily at Big Will.

'*Do it!*' roared Will, his command

making the others jump.

They rushed at Dave, who stood his ground but had to duck as Pierce hurled his gun at his head. Then, with surprising speed, he and Riley gripped Dave's arms, one each. But Dave simply let himself drop as their steely fingers closed on him.

The sudden, unexpected move took the Vandemanns off-guard and both stumbled, instinctively groping at each other for support.

Dave wasn't still for a moment, twisting and ducking and moving his feet, dragging the others off-balance. They collided in a kind of brief, wild dance, stumbling. Dave charged and sent them crashing into Big Will, who was jumping in now, his gun waving wildly.

To everyone's surprise — *shock!* — Big Will ignored the closeness of his brothers and triggered. Pierce yelled and staggered back out of the mêlée, clawing at his face where the powder had scorched his cheek, blistering the edge of one ear. He bellowed in fright and the sound stopped everyone dead in their tracks.

Dave, startled, was first to react. He swung his gun backhanded and it took Riley across the head. He dropped to his knees and grabbed wildly, looking for any support. He wrapped his arms around the thick legs of Big Will and the eldest Vandemann yelled and cussed and swiped and punched, by accident or design, kneeing him in the face. Off-balance, Big Will crashed down on top of the falling Riley and the couple ended up thrashing about on the ground.

Pierce blinked when it happened, started to try to help his kin, but Dave kicked his legs from under him and lunged aside. The Vandemanns were masters of rough-and-tumble brawling and Will hurled Riley into Dave. They collided violently and both fell sprawling. Big Will yelled at men who worked for him to 'Lend a goddamn hand here or there's no pay!'

Three or four hardcases crowded in and Dave elbowed and head-butted, swerved, writhed and kicked, never still for a moment, getting ready to use the gun he still held.

Skin split and blood flowed, curses singed the air. He could barely get enough breath as they reached for him, one man howling as the striking gun smashed bones in his reaching hand. Dave aimed the Colt high and triggered two fast shots. The men scattered and Big Will, just rising to his feet, was knocked sprawling.

After his gun hammer clicked on an empty chamber, Dave ran.

There was a bunch of horses that had been captured in the raid drinking at the small stream that flowed through here, but only one had a saddle.

It was the star-blazed black and Dave didn't hesitate, vaulted into leather, almost toppled off as the horse swung wildly, snorting and half-rearing in fright.

But it had been broken to saddlework

and the rough handling of the Border ranch-hands, so, quickly settled, though snorting a token protest as it responded to Dave's raking, spurless heels.

He rammed it through a not-too-eager group of men who stepped briefly into his path and they dived away in all directions, ignoring Will Vandemann's shouts to '*Stop that son of a bitch!*'

Others were still making up their minds to interfere or not as Dave grabbed the flying reins and wheeled away.

To his surprise, the black actually leapt clear across a narrow part of the stream and then he was crashing through brush and heading upslope, Big Will's curses still ringing in his ears.

'You got three strikes agin you now, Brent! My brothers an' that hoss, goddamn you! I want that black — an' I'll get him an' when I do, I'll ride him over you so many times not even the coyotes'll want to touch you!'

Nice comforting thoughts to help a man sleep easy! Dave allowed, as the black's speed upslope increased with surprising ease. *By God! He might yet make his escape!*

Dave urged the eager horse on, and there was a heap of relief behind the wild shout he gave in mocking farewell.

4

Right or Wrong?

In Case Barlow's law office, Dave paused and shrugged.

'Obviously, I made it.'

Lew Burns glanced at the sheriff and when Barlow remained silent, said, 'Because of a damn good hoss and lots of luck, I'd say.'

'*Lots* of luck,' admitted Dave, watching the sheriff, who seemed ready to speak.

'Why lie about takin' the hoss from — what's his name? Brent . . . ?' He paused. 'Or is it?'

Dave skirted that part as he shrugged. 'Didn't really want to get into the mercenary thing. There's been a lot of trouble over it between the US and Mexico. I might even have a price on my head as one of Rey's mercenaries.'

'Hmmm. Mebbe I'll look into that, but that black must've been somethin' of a bugbear, son.' Dave and Burns both looked puzzled. 'I mean, marked the way he is — blaze on his chest and the tip of one ear, he'd stand out. Specially if they mentioned them things on the dodger — an' I reckon they would've.'

Dave looked sharply at the sheriff. 'Dodger?'

Barlow continued to stare steadily at Dave, nodding very slightly. 'Well, it is a stolen horse.'

'How the hell you make that out?' Dave asked irritably, but thought he knew what was coming.

Barlow spread his small hands, keeping his elbows tucked in close to his body in the gunfighter's way. 'You were ridin' with the Vandemanns for a start an' I'm here to tell you they are not a bunch of men you'd see at Sunday church meetings.'

'Hell! There was no law south of the Rio at that time! We drove Rey's bunch back across the Rio!'

Barlow continued as if Dave hadn't spoken. 'By your own admission, son, you took part in those raids on the Broken K and the Lazy V this side of the Rio. That black was stole from its rightful owner in one of those raids.'

'The ranch owner was dead,' Dave answered flatly. 'And I had nothing to do with those raids. I was over on the neighbouring Fat Snake and found it just about abandoned — some bank had foreclosed a couple days earlier and we hadn't gotten the word. Nearly all those broncs came from Broken K. But you can't steal a horse, or anything else, from a dead man, Sheriff.'

Barlow's tone was clipped, his face set in hard lines. 'You might think that'd be the way of it, but I can quote you at least three legal judgments of cases just like this one: property taken is labelled as 'stolen goods', not 'pickin's', like most folk would think. Thought I'd already mentioned next-of-kin and so on . . . ?'

Burns pursed his lips, looked a mite uncomfortable, watching Dave, who was more than doubtful, though he had heard of lawmen *bending* the law to suit their own purposes. But his main feeling was one of disappointment: he had figured Case Barlow for a man of more integrity.

'I'll admit I've rid both sides of the line now and again, Sheriff, but — '

'What 'line' we talkin' about?' interrupted Barlow curtly, sounding innocent.

'Why, that imaginary one — you know, one side is all law-abidin', the other — well, it kind of lets a man *bend* the rules a little now and then.'

'I got no use for that kinda hogwash!' Barlow snapped and, as he began to say something else, Dave held up a hand and reached for the old battered wallet he had left on Walt Craig and which was now on Barlow's desk with the other meagre belongings taken from the corpse.

'All right if I get something outa this, Sheriff?'

Suspicious, Barlow hesitated, then nodded curtly. He and Burns watched as Dave brought out the folded, creased and somewhat greasy piece of paper he had planted on Craig and shook it out. Burns craned to see as Barlow took it and began to read its contents.

It was a receipt from a Texas Panhandle rancher named Marvin Kennedy.

'He's a blood relative of the dead owner of Broken K,' Dave said quietly. 'First cousin, I believe.'

Barlow looked up sourly, his face like thunder. 'Describes the hoss, all right, blaze marks and all. Says it's in payment for work done by you on the Broken K ranch . . . ?'

'Five months' hard work!' Dave allowed with a trace of bitterness. 'Kennedy is one hard son of a bitch and that was his 'take-it-or-leave-it' offer. I wanted that horse bad so I worked till he said 'nuff'. An' his 'nuff' was way too long in comin', but I liked that horse a helluva lot.' He nodded to the paper. 'You're holdin' Kennedy's receipt for him.'

Burns took the paper from Barlow's unresisting fingers as the lawman continued to glare at Dave.

'I ain't one likes to be made a fool of, mister!'

'No such thing intended, Sheriff! I just — '

'Case!' Burns said suddenly, holding out the paper now. 'The receipt's made out to Dave Brent not Walter P. Craig!'

Barlow kept his face blank and then said, 'You wanna explain that?'

'Nothin' to explain.' Dave paused, knowing he had to finish now. 'I *am* Dave Brent. I planted that receipt on the dead man. He's the real Walter Patrick Craig, of course, but the horse is really mine.'

Air hissed briefly through Burns's teeth and Barlow's eyes slitted. 'Now this is gettin' *right* interestin', but, I b'lieve you have the floor, son, so *keep talkin'*!'

The sheriff added these last two

57

words with his right hand resting on his gun butt and Dave felt a sharp tension in his chest.

'Thought the dead man was s'posed to be this Dave Brent,' added Burns in his quiet, troublemaking way.

'*He*'s Walter Patrick Craig,' Dave cut in curtly, deciding he would need to watch this Burns closely. 'Sheriff, I've rid a thousand miles and more to get away from them damn Vandemanns. They been doggin' me here an' there, seem to have some kinda knack picking up my trail — '

'Sounds like the Vandemanns I know of,' Barlow admitted slowly and Burns said, 'The hell'd you do to them?'

Dave gave him a hard look. 'You heard my story, Lew. In the general schmozzle down there on the Rio I killed two of Will Vandemann's kin — his younger brothers.' He shifted his gaze to the deadpan sheriff. 'I told you they came at me with guns smokin': I had no choice but to shoot back or be killed.'

'Way you told it I'd have to agree with you,' Barlow admitted slowly. 'But then, I ain't heard any of Vandemann's side of things.'

Dave made an exasperated gesture. 'Jesus Christ! They came at me, *shooting*! I just shot back! I didn't know who the hell they were 'till after.'

'Hey, son! Don't get all hot under the collar with me! It's your story.'

'It's the damn truth!' Dave was mad at himself for letting his anger show, but he had a feeling that he could still end up in jail here if Barlow decided that was the thing to do.

So he managed to take a long, deep breath, calmed himself down and told his story with all the details he could remember.

'I've been dodging the sonuvers for almost a year. There's no way I can hope to talk myself out of this trouble. I killed the two young Vandemanns and that's it! Big Will won't even begin to listen to anything else: no matter how it came about, his kin was *killed* and he aims to have my neck if it takes him the rest of his life!'

There was a brief silence, Burns looking to Barlow for a reply, and finally the sheriff said, 'You seem to have a knack for quick thinkin', son.'

Dave shrugged. 'Else it's 'quick and the dead' these days, Sheriff.'

'Yeah,' admitted Burns grudgingly, 'you had bad luck, but what about poor ol' Walt Craig? Any kin he has'll never know what happened to him — if, as you hoped, he'd been found and identified as you.'

Barlow glanced sharply at Burns.

'I see it as a desperation move, Lew — on Brent's part. I savvy *why* he did it, but stealin' someone's identity is worse'n stealing his horse, I reckon.'

Dave almost went for his gun. *This pair would drive him to distraction, teetering and tottering like they were.*

But he couldn't quite find the courage to try to draw against a man with Barlow's reputation.

He looked from one to the other and

said quietly, 'All I figured was planting my stuff on Craig would help get the Vandemanns off my neck and I could get on with my life without looking over my shoulder all the time, expectin' to see Big Will and his kin standing there with guns cocked and ready — or a goddamn lynch rope.'

'Well, you sure picked a bunch of mean ones to keep you awake at night . . . I could bring you to trial in a couple of days and . . . well, you wouldn't want that — it'd be news that'd get back to the Vandemanns and they'd come swarmin' in here and — '

'You enjoyin' this, Barlow?' Dave cut in sharply. 'You *want* to do these things you're threatening me with? Jail, court — or you just got a twisted sense of humour?'

Burns sucked in a sharp breath and even gave a small warning jerk of his head at Dave, who was matching stare-for-stare with Barlow. Dave didn't flinch. But nor did Case . . .

'Stubborn, huh?' he said flatly. 'You

be one of them men born to trouble, I'm thinkin', Dave Brent.'

'Think what you like. It's what you're gonna *do* about it that's bothering me.'

'An' so it should!'

'Well?' Despite himself Dave tensed and his right hand twitched a little — then he actually jumped — *staring down the barrel of the Smith & Wesson pistol held in the gnarled hand of Case Barlow. He'd never seen such gunspeed* — never! He found his own gunhand was now dangling limply at his side, well away from his Colt.

'Case! Easy, man!' Burns said shakily. 'Judas! I thought he was a goner!'

'*You* thought I was a goner!' breathed Dave keeping his nervousness under control, but added quickly, 'No gunplay intended, Sheriff.'

'Better not be.' Barlow muttered the words and Dave thought he saw a small tremor in the man's hand as he deftly holstered the Smith & Wesson. There were beads of sweat on his wrinkled brow. 'Sometimes I kinda forget that

I'm wearin' a badge and tend to settle things the old way.'

'They're settled, as far as I'm concerned, Sheriff. Any way you decide.' Dave's thudding heart crashed against his ribs. 'Mebbe I did wrong, but — '

'Yeah, yeah you did wrong, but, like I said, I can savvy *why*. Might've been tempted to do likewise under the same circumstances. Well now, where do we stand?'

'We got Craig's body, Case, some-thin's gonna have to be done about that.' Burns pinched his nostrils lightly, grimacing.

Barlow frowned. 'You're right. Arrange for Norbert Bright to bury him.' He glanced at Dave. 'Some name for an undertaker, huh? Lew, I'm puttin' you back on full pay as deputy till I get this out of the way. Think Doris'll fuss over that?'

Lew Burns was looking a little unsure. 'I reckon it'll be all right, but I'll be watchin' my grub for ground glass, just the same! She warned me about takin' the deputy badge full-time again . . . but we can use the money.' He lifted a finger in Dave's direction. 'Thanks, Brent!'

He half-grinned and adjusted his hat and made for the door. Dave turned to the lawman. 'Am I free to go or what?'

'Well, I dunno as I've decided that, son. Look, I'll come clean with you: I'll be sixty-six come fall. My contract was s'posed to run out when I turned sixty-five but this town wanted me to stick around and I obliged.' He lowered his voice. 'Fact is I got no savin's for all the big money I've earned. But I got a wife who's been' — he paused, then lifted a finger and twirled it briefly above one temple, looking mighty embarrassed — ' 'poorly' might fit. Ever since our young daughter died. Late-life baby. Sometimes I think it woulda been better if Millie hadn't come through the birth.' He coughed and his face straightened out. 'What I'm sayin' is, son, you're plumb outa luck.'

Dave looked carefully at the old lawman. 'How so?'

'If I prove to this town council I still got some of the old spark in me, they'll keep me in office for another year and — ' He coughed again, wheezing, using a crumpled kerchief to cover his mouth. 'And Doc says Millie will just about last that long. Then, well, I won't care what happens to me after that.'

He paused and Dave sat there, face taut. 'Sheriff, I'm truly sorry to hear about your troubles, but I don't see how *I'm* involved.'

Barlow smiled crookedly. 'Now, come on, son, you ain't that dumb! You know what I gotta do.'

'Now, listen!' Dave stood abruptly, careful to keep his gun arm still. '*I've done you no harm — nor Walt Craig!* You can't charge me with anything — '

Again he stopped dead as the Smith & Wesson's barrel peeped over the edge of the desk, angled toward him.

'Son, I am locking you up until I've looked some more into your story.

Could take a little time to check things out, but if your story's true then — '

'You can't do this to me!'

Barlow smiled again, not much more than a twitch of the lips, and Dave knew damn well the old gunfighter *could* and *would* do exactly what he wanted.

* * *

And it sure didn't help any when he was woken in his cell in the middle of the night and told that Norbert Bright, the town undertaker, while preparing Craig's body for burial, found definite signs that the man had been tortured pretty damn thoroughly before he died.

'Tortured?' Dave's sleep-drugged mind made him slur the word. 'The-the hell you say!'

'That's right,' chipped in Lew Burns, standing holding the lantern for Case Barlow and looking grim. 'Burn marks, cuts, bruises. We're all wonderin' just what you got him to tell you before you threw him in the river to drown.'

'Except he was already dead when you dropped him in,' said Barlow coldly. 'Norb Bright found hardly any water in his lungs. You got a murder to try and talk yourself out of, son. Reckon you can do it?'

5

Rat Hole

There was no more sleep for Dave that night.

The cell wasn't as small as some he'd seen — and been in — but it wasn't all that large, either. He could walk seven paces side to side, and about four from the door to the bunk and bucket.

He gripped the bars of the door more than once, starting to rattle it, but the sound did something to him, actually brought him back to what he liked to think was 'normal'.

Once, he'd been in a cell next to a man who'd never been in jail before and — he'd forgotten what the man was charged with — he screamed his innocence, *cried* until he was dried out. Dave had tried to calm him with words but he ended up bad-mouthing Dave, shook that door until the exasperated lawmen came and knocked him out with a gun butt, took him away and put him in an isolation cell where he'd finally managed to hang himself with one leg ripped off his trousers and knotted high around the barred doors.

There was little danger of Dave going to such extremes. But that picture had stayed with him for years — especially since the very next day, some drifter, dying of a gunshot wound, had confessed to the crime the youngster had been charged with.

Such thoughts did little to relax Dave now.

He must have drifted off into a kind of a sleep sometime because the jail trusty, a wife-beater, tearfully contrite now that he had sobered up, brought him breakfast as grey daylight trickled through the bars of the window.

The food was surprisingly good and Dave cleaned the plate, looked up and was surprised to find the trusty still standing outside the door.

'You waitin' for this?' Dave turned the empty plate sideways and offered it through the bars. The trusty took it languidly, looked at Dave, who noticed the man's eyes were full of tears.

'I-I never meant to hurt her!' he said, with a kind of sob. 'I-I just drank too much . . . '

Dave suddenly felt sorry for him in his pathetic hangdog remorse. 'How bad?'

'Huh? Oh, black eye — an' — I tore her best frock up. Aw, shoot! I was just a mean bastard! I-I'm ashamed to go home.' He slammed himself on the forehead with the heel of his free hand. 'Mean! Mean! Mean! Poor Rose, she didn't deserve that — not from me.'

'You got any money?'

The man blinked. 'Only what Case gives me for this chore — 'bout a week's worth owin'. I asked him to hold it so I won't be tempted to start drinkin' again . . . '

'Get it and buy her a new dress and a hairdo. Take her out to a diner for supper — and give her a red rose — that'll likely do it.'

The trusty stared, mouth agape, then closed it and gulped. 'You really think it'll work?'

'Well, I ain't had much experience with wives but yeah, I reckon it's worth a try.'

The man suddenly grinned. 'Me too! Oh, hell yeah! Worth a damn good try.'

He practically ran down the passage just as the block door opened and Lew Burns — now with his deputy's badge pinned to his vest — signed for Dave to come out.

'The hell's the matter with you, Burt?' he asked without any real interest as the trusty pushed by and ran off. Burns grunted. 'C'mon, Brent . . . out!' He held his six-gun in his right hand. 'Case is ready for you now.'

Dave lifted red eyes. 'Mebbe I'm not ready for him.'

Burns chuckled. 'You better be! C'mon! Move!'

Barlow, at his desk, was mopping the

last of the egg yolk from a plate as they entered. He swallowed the lump of bread, picked up a steaming cup and sipped, watching Dave all the time.

'Hope you had a miserable night, son,' was his greeting to Dave. 'Can't abide anyone who can sit and watch another man suffer from the things he's doin' to him. It don't cut no ice with me, mister! You're scum, in my book.'

'I never tortured Craig, Barlow,' Dave said heavily. 'He was dead when I found him . . . I told you my story and I'm not changing it, because it's the way it happened.'

'And you just never noticed all them burns an' knife cuts?' Burns said coldly. 'Your story stinks, feller!'

'So does your logic!' Dave retorted. 'Hell, you've both seen Craig's corpse. I never touched it except to take his wallet and find out who he was. Christ, he was battered and bruised and cut up, sure! But I reckoned that was from when he washed down over the upstream rapids, nearly half a damn mile of jagged rocks! Mebbe the undertaker would notice burns and so on, but I never even looked that close. I got a pretty strong stomach, but I didn't want to have Craig around any longer than I had to . . . he was already getting ripe.'

The lawmen exchanged looks and Dave thought there might have been some doubt starting to show on Burns's flat features. Barlow's were unreadable, his eyes like tombstones in this early light.

'Thing is, son, we'd like to know what'd make one man do them things to another. Sure, you wanted somethin' from him. Had to be information, I guess. Well, we'd like to know *what the hell that information was!*'

'I've told you what happened,' Dave said wearily.

'Goddammit, Brent!' snapped Lew Burns. 'We're not fools! Why, hell, there wouldn't be another lawman with the kinda reputation Case's got within five hundred miles! He's smart! You ever think of that? He din' get this far just by bein' faster with a gun than anyone else — he's got *brains*, feller, and you are one sorry son of a bitch if you think you can hornswoggle him in any way!'

Dave stared silently for a moment, then said, 'How about you? You hornswoggle easy?'

Burns's eyes widened as deep colour surged into his face, darkening it. He lunged at Dave and punched him while Dave still sat in his chair, hands in cuffs. The blow knocked him sprawling to the floor.

'Ease up there, Lew!' Barlow said lazily and tossed a meaningless half-smile at Dave as he struggled to his feet, blood trickling from one corner of his mouth. 'Sorry, Brent. Wasn't quick enough to stop him — but he's a loyal ol' hoss, an' I do appreciate his opinion of me. *Gracias*, ol' pard.'

Lew Burns still looked angry and nodded curtly. 'What the hell we gonna do with this sonuver, Case?'

'Aw, I dunno. He's been caught with

his pants down, so to speak. Nearly had us — 'hornswoggled' was it, you said?' He chuckled. 'Haven't heard that expression in a 'coon's age . . . but, yeah! Gettin' right down to it, we're duty-bound to find out why he treated Walter Craig so bad.' He lifted his cup, sipped, grimaced, and murmured, '*Damn! Cold!*'

Then dashed the remains into his prisoner's face.

Dave reared back, spluttering, eyes stinging, the chair rocking and teetering. Barlow nodded gently.

Burns came over fast and kicked the legs of Dave's chair from under him. He crashed to the floor, timber splintering, cursing as it drew blood from his cheek and nose.

The deputy leaned over the dazed prisoner, gun in hand now. 'We'll let them coupla marks on your face stay, Brent. But we don't want a lot of such things showin', so any more — like *this*!' He kicked Dave solidly in the ribs, skidding him away from the broken chair. 'Or — *this*!' A repeat performance of the kick. 'Will be where they won't show so easy, but you'll sure feel 'em! Savvy?'

Dave writhed and gagged, almost lost his breakfast. Then Burns grabbed his shirt collar and heaved him into a corner, propped up against the walls, bleeding, dazed — still cuffed. *He had been in better situations . . .*

No one spoke for a while — except once, when Burns snapped at Dave to be still.

Puffing on one of his potent cheroots, Barlow said, 'Thought you'd like to tell us what you was tryin' to get outa poor ol' Craig, son, but guess you're dumber'n I figured. You oughta know by now what I'm waitin' to hear.'

Dave snorted in a brief parody of a laugh — or was it a sneer? 'I know what you'd *like* to hear from me, but there ain't a thing I can tell you, except to say one more time that I nev — '

Dave stopped abruptly as Burns leaned over him and placed the blade foresight of his six-gun under Dave's left eye, the cold metal digging into the meagre flesh. 'Don't say it! You do, one more time, and I'll rip your eye out!'

Dave blinked, tears oozing into the distorted socket. Burns's face was an out-of-focus blur but his voice had a lot of persuasion in it.

Dave was breathing hard, mouth dry, stomach knotted, as the foresight kept digging in.

'He — he never said nothin'!' Dave grated.

There was a hint of triumph in Burns's face as he glanced at Barlow. 'An' the mayor's wife and her 'committee' say guns oughta be banned. That they're no help to anyone.'

Barlow merely continued to stare down at Dave, looking thoughtful. 'I ain't sure our friend here is bein' truthful, Lew. How about it, Dave? You just stallin'?'

Dave felt a slight increase in pressure of the gunsight under his eye, licked his lips, and spoke in as steady a voice as he could manage under the circumstances.

'Craig never said anything — *'cause I never tortured him! He was already dead when I found him!*'

He not only wrenched his head quickly to the side, he used his legs to push away from the wall, falling flat on his back — even so the gunsight tore a red streak across his forehead, eyebrow to hairline: but he'd saved his eye.

Burns swore, almost overbalanced and thrust up, managing to kick the prostrate Dave in the stomach before Barlow's crisp voice stopped him.

'Hate to admit it, Lew, but I'm gettin' to where I just *might* start believin' this *hombre*.'

Burns glared. 'Gimme ten minutes in the special cell, Case, and I'll soon have the truth outa him.'

'No. No, I think I need more before I decide.'

That obviously didn't suit Burns, but he swallowed any sharp retort he might have considered making.

'You ain't forgotten who Craig was?' Burns asked tentatively and the cold, frowning look the sheriff gave him made him nod quickly. 'No — no. 'Course you ain't. I was just talkin', Case.'

'Well, watch what you say! And *when*!' Barlow snapped. He let the look linger a moment, then leaned over the still prostrate Dave Brent. 'You see how it's gonna be, don't you, son? You keep lyin' to us and we keep workin' on you until we might's well hand over what's left to Norb Bright. You'll be out of it by then and we'll still be clenchin' our teeth just wonderin' what was so damn important that you'd rather die than tell us.' He shook his head slowly. 'I gotta admit I'm *damned* puzzled, an' I'm a man who hates a mystery. I'll do almost anythin' to find out what it is . . . ' He looked up and smiled coldly. 'Hell! that ain't quite right. *I will do anythin'* — anythin' at all — *to find out!*'

'How about I shoot off one of his toes, Case?' Burns asked. 'We can always say it was an accident. That Brent done it himself, tryin to fumble his own gun out an' . . . '

'Now that seems like a possibility, Lew! I kinda like that.' Case Barlow looked soberly into Dave's face. 'But not just now.'

'Aw, hell, Case! We can — '

One level look from Barlow and Lew Burns shut up.

'We got Mr Brent here where we can call on him whenever we need to, Lew. We'll just let him have some time to hisself. Time to *think*! We'll put him where it's nice and quiet, where he won't be disturbed.'

'The isolation cell!' Burns said suddenly, smiling now. 'Hell, yeah! That's perfect, Case.'

'Not for everyone,' Barlow said, with a crooked grin as he stared into Dave's face. 'But then we ain't here to please everyone, are we?'

'I should smile we ain't!'

Lew Burns couldn't keep from laughing and Dave didn't like the sound of it — not one little bit.

★　★　★

Isolation was right.

It was little more than a hole in the rock wall underneath the main jailhouse with a heavily barred door across the only opening. No, not quite the only opening — the only visible one, yes, but there was a draught of cold air, bearing a hint of dust and trees, sweeping through, kind of damp, too, so there must be some kind of vent up there above. Whatever it was, it was high in the roof and not as wide as a small child's shoulders.

'You won't die from lack of air,' Burns assured Dave with a twisted smile, holding the oil lamp up so the prisoner could see the narrow bunk with ratty-looking, no doubt bug-infested, blanket. There was a hole in the floor in place of a slop bucket and the stench was stomach-churning.

'Bixby's a well-established town,' the

deputy added. 'In the early days there was lots of trouble from the Injuns: Arapaho, Cheyenne — a few Blackfeet even comin' down from Canada — so what the settlers did, when they got fed up with 'em, was grab the chief or medicine man and lock him up down here.'

Dave waited when Burns paused — he knew something more was coming. Burns chuckled.

'Them old settlers! By God, wish we had as free a hand as they did, handlin' outlaws but only the odd Injun, nowadays. When they had 'em down here, them pioneers, they left a couple to actually *rot* down here. You might even see their bones, you game enough to stick your head over that there hole!' He laughed, genuinely amused. 'Could even hear their ghosts!'

'I never did believe in ghosts,' Dave said and the remark earned him a backhand across the face.

'Shut up!' Burns snapped. 'I ain't gonna leave you no kinda light! No lamp, or candle stub. Nothin'! How you like that? Ain't afraid of the dark, are you?'

'Not since I was a kid.' Dave's words were slurred and he spat a little blood.

'You'll soon quit that smart talk, Brent! We'll just let you stew a while and see if you can remember what you tortured outa Mr Walter P. Craig.'

'I tell you I never — ' Dave jumped back just in time to save his fingers, where they gripped the bars, from being crushed by Burns's swinging gun barrel.

'You'll change your mind! No food, no one to talk to, nothin' to look at 'cept the rats! See how long you last.'

'I got some kinda record to beat?'

'Well, yeah! Now you mention it — we had a buffalo skinner we suspected was smugglin' stolen gold out with his skins. Never did catch him at it, but he lasted — aw, how long was it? Lemme see if I can recall — *yeah!* Three days! Then he spilled his guts. Figure you can beat that?'

'Come back in four days and ask me.'

'Judas, I'd love to put a bullet in you, you smart-talkin' son of a bitch! But Case is runnin' things and I ain't stupid enough to go up agin *him*! Sleep tight, Brent!'

Burns turned up the lantern flame as he prepared to move off, began whistling softly.

'What makes Walt Craig so important, anyway?'

The whistling stopped abruptly and the lantern showed Burns's anger-tight face as he whirled. 'Judas Priest, Brent! I'm so close to puttin' a bullet in you that — that — '

'You'd even risk the wrath of Barlow?' Dave asked.

For a moment he thought he'd gone just that little bit too far as Burns brought up his six-gun and cocked it. But he didn't shoot, only bad-mouthed Dave until the prisoner said tiredly, 'You ain't got much imagination, Burns. I heard all them names before I run away from school!'

It was close. He could hear the snorting breaths gusting through Burns's flared nostrils.

Then the man took control of himself, let go one more epithet, turned, and headed for the door, taking the lantern with him.

'Well, it's just that I'm damned if I could savvy what Craig was talkin' about. Made no sense to me.'

Burns stopped abruptly, turning, gun in one hand as he held the lantern high enough for light to just reach Dave at the bars.

'So he did talk!'

Dave tried to sound as if he wished he hadn't spoken, but nodded with a kind of sad sigh. Burns was on edge, eyes bright, figuring he had Dave where he wanted him now, came striding back to the bars, looking mighty mean.

'Could hardly make him out,' Dave murmured. 'Too much pain, I guess. He was kinda sobbing when he gave up . . .'

'Jesus! Case was right: you are scum!'

'You don't think you're the only ones knew about Craig, do you?'

Burns came closer, holding up the lantern, studying Dave's face through the rust-flaking bars. After a short time he grunted, 'What d'*you* know about him? Hell! I ain't so sure Craig *did* tell you anythin'.'

'Well, you'll never know, will you?'

'You reckon? Judas, man, I been around Injuns long enough to know some of their ways. I could have you spillin' your guts in five minutes maximum!'

Dave snorted. 'Lots of luck!'

Burns stepped right up to the bars and raised his gun, thumbing back the hammer. 'You only have to live long enough to tell me what Craig said. Once you do that . . . ' The deputy shrugged. 'Got no more use for you. *But!* I could do a deal. Trade you a quick bullet instead of all that pain that's comin' your way. Case would want to talk to you first, just to make sure you ain't bluffin'. And whatever you done to Craig'll seem like a kid's party game. Worth thinkin' about?'

Dave stepped back — a half-step was about all there was room for. But he looked mighty worried.

'Aw, come on!' He made his voice quaver a little. 'I tell you what you wanta know, you'll owe me enough to let me go! Judas, that's fair, ain't it?'

Burns laughed out loud, shaking his head. 'Man, have you got *gall*! Why — '

Dave's right arm shot between the bars, grabbed at the waving gun and clamped down on the cylinder so it couldn't fire because it was unable to turn. As Burns staggered, Dave smashed the man's gunhand back into his face and broke his nose, blood spurting.

Burns's legs sagged and Dave twisted his fingers in the deputy's hair and yanked him face-first into the iron bars. Twice.

This time Burns's legs gave way and he sprawled on the damp ground, moaning, bleeding head pressed up against the bars.

Dave was breathing heavily as he strained to move the deputy's body closer so he could feel in the man's pockets for the keys. In the process, he pulled the gun between the bars and rested it against his bent leg where he could reach it fast if he had to.

There were seven keys on the ring he found in one of his trouser pockets. None looked like it would fit the ancient door lock, but then he noticed one with a bright streak of metal showing through a coating of rust — a key that hadn't been used as much as those for the other cells . . . until recently? He was right, and in moments stood free. He dragged the deputy into the cramped, stinking cell, stripped him of his gunbelt, took all his money, even took his tobacco sack and papers and, finally — the man's shirt.

Dave's had been torn and soiled earlier. Burns gave a moan and Dave was glad to hear it: he thought at first he might have killed him. The shirt fitted well enough and he locked the door, tossed the keys down the sewage shaft and made his way carefully up the narrow twisting stairs cut into the rock to the jailhouse above, the six-gun cocked.

He hadn't even known if it was still daylight or dark down in that stinking hell.

But it was dark. The law office was empty, a small lamp burning on Case Barlow's desk — but no sign of the sheriff — for which Dave felt relief. *Burns must've had first guard duty for the night.*

He found his own rifle and Colt in a cupboard, went out the back way into a small dark yard with a set of stables and found the black horse inside. It greeted him with a small whinny which he quickly stifled by cupping his hand over the muzzle while he stroked the animal and spoke quietly. His saddle was in a corner and he threw it on the horse quickly, watching and listening for any sign of Case Barlow.

But the man would likely be at supper now. *Hell, it didn't matter where he was, as long as he wasn't here!*

He led the horse into a lane that ran behind the jailhouse, mounted, and cleared town after running into a few dead-ends and a lot of twisting and turning. He hadn't had time to look around and get his bearings earlier.

The horse was eager to run and he let it have its head, allowed it to pick its own way up the mountain trail behind Bixby.

He would find a safe place to hole up for the night, rise with the sun and pick a high ridge where he could see what the country was like and — hopefully — get clear — and stay clear.

He had a notion Case Barlow's orders would be to '*Shoot on sight!*'

No, wait!

The sheriff wouldn't want him killed: first he would want to find out what Walter P. Craig had — supposedly — told Dave under torture.

And Dave had a notion that Case Barlow wouldn't be above applying a little torture of his own if that's what it took to get what he wanted.

6

Rough Country

There was no moon and the stars were masked by a thin layer of cloud which might mean rain was in the offing.

Dave was almost fighting the black now — there was no real trail and the ground was not only broken and scattered with apple-sized rocks, but there was a layer of loose gravel, which, combined with the steepness, caused the horse to stumble many times.

Dave had always respected his mounts' instincts and realized he was in such a hurry now to shake this country that that was one thing he wasn't doing.

The black was shaking its head, and pawing the ground, even gave a short whinny!

That was the last thing Dave wanted. He leaned forward in the saddle, patted the arched, throbbing neck and spoke gently into the flicking ear. The black made a brief, rumbling grunt which Dave recognized as its way of saying: *You're the one made the mistake — try again.*

Dave briefly patted the black's neck, nudged with his heels and slackened off the reins.

The horse immediately moved left and Dave almost hauled back on the reins again, but — *No! Let the black work at it his way for a while.*

It seemed a lot longer than Dave wanted to spend on the face of the mountain but they were making better progress down the steep slope.

Then, both horse and man panting audibly, they came to a break in the trees and he looked down on a dim landscape and even a glint of the river, winding far ahead.

He was surprised that he was still within sight of that damn river! But the mountains obviously curved and he hadn't noticed as the black struggled under him, following its senses, looking for the best way to go.

He dismounted, punched in his hat's crown and gave the horse a small amount of water from his canteen and drank himself. Then he squatted on a rock, eyes more used to the darkness now, and very carefully studied what lay ahead.

The only conclusion he came to was this was mighty rough country and there was a hell of a lot of it.

The sooner he got moving again the better.

He knew a posse couldn't be organized for some time yet — at least until somehow Burns made himself heard, yelling for help in that hellhole — but he figured any posse would be made up of men who knew this land like their own back yards.

And the word would be to take him alive which meant they would shoot first at the black, set him afoot!

Dave didn't mind being afoot so much, the army had taught him how to live off the country and to stay well hidden, but he cringed inwardly at the thought of the black being killed outright, or, worse, wounded, left crippled.

'*The hell with it!*' He didn't aim for that to happen.

So he found a way over and down and this time the black allowed him to do the guiding, veering away from steep drops — two of which Dave saw almost too late in this lousy bug-humming darkness amongst the trees.

Then, when he figured he must be about halfway down the slope with most of the mountain between him and Bixby, the moon came out. Just like that — the murky layer of cloud disappeared and within seconds there was enough light to see by. It was still weak but it allowed him to move faster and within twenty minutes he was down on flat, brush-covered land again and close enough to the river to hear it gurgling and chuckling over stones.

He was lying prone, just upstream

from the horse, both drinking sparingly, Dave dousing his head, when the first shot blasted out of the night and the bullet caromed off one of the bigger stones, splashing him with water.

With a grunt he rolled away, dragging the reins of the black, which came willingly enough and he vaulted into the saddle. He lay low along its neck as he let it run into thicker cover — but not thick enough.

There were four more shots before he ran the black into another clump of trees, but he straightened too quickly and was rammed from the saddle by a low branch. He struggled to swing up again but fumbled his hold on the stirrup and skidded flatbellied as the horse shied away.

The hell was this? Dave's mind screamed as he dived behind a low bush with spiky branches which dug into him in a dozen places. He had the six-gun in hand, now, wishing the black was closer so he could leap up and drag his rifle from the saddle scabbard.

But the main thought was: *Why should he have to?*

There was no way Barlow could have set up a posse yet! No way! There was no telegraph running across the mountain, though he realized he could be in the next county here — the mountain range forming the boundary line. But the fact remained: Barlow could not have contacted anyone this side of the range so soon and yet he heard enough to know there were at least three or more men hunting him. Maybe as many as six.

Hell almighty! What kind of lousy luck was dogging him now? The black had run off — not that he blamed it, but —

'Get below him to the draw, Hank!' a voice yelled, a man's strained voice, as if its owner had been running or climbing. 'Kel! Kel? You there?'

No answer, and Dave Brent found out why in about ten seconds because 'Kel', whoever he might be, dropped off a low ridge and landed right beside him, swinging a rifle. It was cramped and awkward in the space, otherwise Dave might have gotten a split skull or worse. But the barrel skidded off his shoulder and banged him over his left ear, making his head swim.

There was enough force in the blow to knock him flat again but his fighting instincts took over and he spun onto his back, drew up his legs swiftly in time to catch the attacking Kel somewhere in the midriff.

The man gagged and rolled to one side, his rifle whiplashing and drooping in his weakened grip. Dave kicked out and it was a lucky kick, taking the smoking rifle out of the other's hands as that same voice as before cried out:

'*Kel!* Jesus, man! Don't kill him yet!'

Kel tried to answer but Dave kicked him in the chest and he did no more than grunt loudly.

It was Dave who called out, breathlessly, 'He said back off, because my gun's at his head! Who the hell are you?'

There was a dead silence, though it didn't last long.

'Who are *you*?' the voice asked with genuine puzzlement. 'It don't sound like Morg Longstreet!'

'Who the hell's Morg Longstreet?' called back Dave, carefully keeping his Colt pressed against the other man's head. The rifle was somewhere underfoot now and Dave felt around for it with his boots as he spoke.

'It ain't him, Josh!' Kel called, voice cracking. 'But he's still got his damn gun borin' into my ear.'

'Then you better ease it off, Mr Whoever-you-are!'

'The hell with you! I got no argument with you fellers. Just tryin' to find a place to bed down for the night.'

'Kinda early to bed, ain't you, feller?' the voice answered cynically. 'What you think, Kel?'

'Told you all I know. It ain't Morg! Christ, mister! Can you move your goddamn gun? My ear feels like a hoss kicked it.'

Dave eased up on the pressure. His foot had located Kel's rifle now and he stood on it, giving his prisoner a shake. 'The hell're you fellers doing in here, shooting at anything that moves?'

Kel didn't answer until Dave bored the gun muzzle into his ear again and he yelled. 'Morg — Morg Longstreet — he's been sparkin' Josh's wife and we almost caught the snake tonight. He run for the mountain and me and Josh an' Hank Ivey come after him. We thought you was him — an' just who the hell are you, anyway?'

'Never mind. Just take it I ain't this Morg feller. All I'm trying to do is find my way outa these mountains.'

'Where you from?' someone asked suddenly. The nearness of the voice startled Dave and he whirled but kept his gun rammed into Kel's chest.

'Judas! If that's you, Josh, you move mighty nice.'

The unexpected compliment brought a belated chuckle from 'Josh'. 'Better b'lieve it, feller. You ain't Morg, I know that, but you ain't said just who the hell you *are*.'

Dave hesitated: these men were from this country, neighbour to Barlow's county, and it wasn't likely there had been any word gotten across yet about the trouble in Bixby.

'I'm just a drifter passin' through. Thought I had enough light to get across this mountain after I'd had an early supper in Bixby. But guess I was wrong. Where am I, anyway?'

'You're in Hammer County here. We ain't very big an' kinda share the Bixby County Seat when we got to but . . . ' Josh paused, as if deciding whether to continue what he was going to say. 'You know the sheriff there is Case Barlow?'

Dave hesitated, then nodded, realized these men might not have seen the gesture and grunted instead.

'Well, I guess that could mean anythin'!' Josh allowed, and Kel muttered something that was apparently in agreement. 'You see, there's a kinda pass, few miles nor'west that all us locals use, from both counties. Wonder Barlow din' tell you about it. Or Lew Burns.'

Dave knew what the man was asking: *was he on the run?* And he had to make a decision because he could just hear someone else coming up behind him and then felt the nudge of what might be a shotgun's muzzle roughly caressing his spine. 'Hey! Easy there!'

But there had been something in Josh's voice whenever he mentioned Barlow — not exactly distasteful, but not hero-worshipping like everyone else who spoke of the old sheriff, either.

'I had no reason to stick around Bixby. Didn't find the sheriff, or his deputy, specially helpful, so I decided to light out after supper — er — I thought Case Barlow was second only to God Himself up this way?'

A silence dragged on for several long seconds.

'Well, we ain't exactly hardcases, but then again we ain't entirely a God-fearin' community neither. Long as

Barlow keeps to his own county, he can be King of England for all we care. Long as he leaves us to run things our way.'

Dave said nothing. It was obvious they were expecting some kind of reply, though, and the increased pressure of the shotgun seemed to emphasize this.

'Barlow don't have any dodgers on me,' he said finally. Then, as the silence still dragged on, added, 'Fact, I was kinda disappointed in Case after all I'd heard about him.'

It was Kel who sighed, sounding genuinely regretful. 'Case was a holy terror a few years back . . . but fair, always fair, with even the real hard-cases. Then, despite his age, he got his wife pregnant, she was years younger'n him. Baby died and she went kinda — funny — an', though he won't admit it, so did he.'

'He told me something about that.'

'He did? Well, you were privileged 'less you knew him from someplace else? No? Case went downhill. He'd led a rough life and it started to catch up with him, rheumatics, lungs tearin' apart from them damn cheroots. An' he couldn't help his wife: it changed him. He's a bitter man now and you wouldn't want to cross him. Vindictive an' mean as a gut-shot grizzly — an', I b'lieve, really pissed at himself for bein' that way. Seems unable to change.'

'Enough of the damn history lesson!' Josh snapped suddenly. 'You, mister, you run afoul of Case? Now we want the truth!'

Dave remained silent while he thought about it, but the shotgun barrel rapped him on the head hard enough to drive him to his knees and the man wielding it spoke in a gravelly voice. 'You gotta speak up, feller. I'm kinda deef and I din' catch one word you said! Try again, huh?'

'Take it easy, damn you!' Dave growled, as Kel helped him to his feet.

'Josh's wife happens to be kin of mine!' the shotgunner growled and Kel stepped in with, 'He ain't the feller been sparkin' her, Hank! Y'ask me, Morg Longstreet's well an' truly gone by now.'

'Bastard better be! He shows his face around here again an' he's gonna be talkin' soprano!' Josh said grimly. Then, suddenly making a decision, 'No, I think this feller's square enough, but I aim to hear why he quit Bixby and come over this here mountain. No one comes this way.'

Dave nodded slowly. 'All right. You fellers know about a man named Walt Craig?'

'That sonuver!' snorted the shotgunner. 'You won't find any friends here if you ran with him, mister!'

'No, never knew him. But I found his body foulin' the river.' He pointed vaguely back over the mountain and went on to give a brief outline of his own story and 'acquaintance' with Craig. He paused and the impatient shotgunner jabbed him in the ribs.

'Will you put that damn thing away?' Dave snapped, but the gun only moved back a few inches. 'Yeah, Barlow turned Craig's body over to the Bixby undertaker and he found what he reckoned were signs of torture.'

Dave told it briefly and there was yet another silence while they considered his story.

'If they put you in that old underground cell where they used to kill the Injuns,' Josh said slowly, 'how'd you get out? Never heard of anyone doin' that.'

'Me and Burns talked it over, kinda swapped places.'

He jumped when both Kel and Josh roared with laughter.

'Now *that* I would've liked to've seen!' allowed Hank, slowly lowering the shotgun. 'I sure would've!'

Dave began to relax: he had taken a chance that these men weren't all that enamoured of Case Barlow and Lew Burns and it seemed as if it had paid off.

'If it's true,' said Josh slowly, and waited until Dave said, 'Now you wouldn't want to call me a liar, would you?'

'Why?'

'Could be . . . dangerous.'

'Aw, I dunno, Josh. He did sound kinda genuine,' Kel said slowly. 'Burns give you much trouble?'

'Not as much as he wanted to,' Dave replied and they let it go at that.

'Then you're gonna have a price on your head, feller. The hell *is* your name anyway?'

Dave told them and, briefly, why there had been a falling-out with the Bixby lawmen. 'They like my hoss but it ain't for sale. Not that they offered to buy — '

'Uh-huh,' said Kel. 'But I'd say that while the hoss might've been part of the issue, I figure Case and Lew would be more interested in findin' out *why* Craig was tortured.'

'*I* didn't torture him!' Dave said flatly. 'I told you that.'

'Ease up, ease up,' urged Josh. 'Just what d'you know about Walt Craig?'

'Whatever I've told you. I found him floatin', dead. Swapped some identification with him because of some fellers who've been doggin' me, and turned him adrift. My bad luck he got washed down among them kids and Lew Burns was within call.'

'You usually that unlucky?' asked Hank, and there was scepticism plain in his words.

'No,' Dave answered shortly, but there was a tone in that brief word that told the shotgunner he could take it further if he wanted to — at his own risk.

Hank wasn't fazed: after all he was the one holding the shotgun only a foot from Dave's head.

'No use goin' into detail, Hank,' Kel said shortly. 'This *hombre*'s story isn't one he could've made up on the spur of the moment. I'm inclined to believe him. How about you, Josh?'

Josh grunted non-committally and Hank shrugged. 'Well, what we gonna do with him?'

'Nothin'!' snapped Dave. 'I've got nothin' to do with your business. Let me get my hoss and you show me a quick way outa these damn hills, I'd be obliged — and you'll never see or hear of me again if I can help it.'

Hank and Kel both looked at Josh, who stared hard through the dim light at Dave and finally said, 'You never seen Walt Craig before you found him in the river, huh?'

Dave sighed. 'Never knew the son of a bitch and I'm beginning to wish I'd never even *heard* of him!' He sensed they still weren't sure if he was telling the truth and they didn't really want to let it go at that. 'Look, what the hell is it about Craig? I thought his injuries were from being rolled down over those rapids, but Barlow and Burns seem to think I beat him up that way. The undertaker — Bright? — he reckons he found so many burns and knife cuts in places they'd make even a Bible-bangin' preacher renounce his calling if someone was workin' on him.'

'Well, he could've, I guess, preparin' Craig for burial,' allowed Hank slowly. 'He'd work close enough . . . '

Dave agreed. 'Sure, but Barlow and Burns not only didn't believe I hadn't done it, seemed to me they didn't want to believe he hadn't been tortured. To me, that means they figure Craig must've had some information that *someone* who got it out of him would benefit from. How'm I doin', fellers? Close?'

Josh nodded slowly. 'Pretty sharp on the uptake, mister.'

'Only way it could be because *I didn't torture him! Hell, I'm tired of sayin' this!'* When no one said anything, Dave added irritably, 'For Chris'sakes! What the hell's the big mystery about Walter goddamn Patrick Craig, anyway?'

It fell to Josh to answer. 'How long you down in that Border country?'

'Couple, three years.'

'Long enough to miss out on what was developin' back here in the good ol' *Unidos Estados*, huh?' He didn't wait for Dave to reply. 'Stagecoaches and railroads were openin' up this country — not the only things, but the most important — 'cause they carried settlers and freight, includin' gold and cash, and all the other things needed to get new towns on their feet. Banks were bustin' at the seams.'

Josh kind of let that drift off, but Dave didn't say anything.

''Course, there was lots of attempts at stealin' all that cash — big temptation — so it needed big escorts travellin' point-to-point.' He squinted more closely at Dave. 'You ever in the army?'

'Towards the end of the war.'

'Not in peacetime? No? OK, then you wouldn't've knowed Craig there.'

'I never knew him at all. Only as a corpse!'

'OK! Christ, quit yellin'! All right. All that money come from Fort McCracken and had to travel over the Big Tablecloth — you know that?'

'Biggest salt desert in North-west

Colorado!' Dave said, with some surprise. 'Why the hell'd the army take that route?'

'Thought you knew the army! One of them things, I guess. Some lollypop general got the idea it was good training for the cavalry, or somethin', I dunno — it don't matter. They used that trail anyway and somehow or other Walt Craig got to lead nearly all the money caravans.'

'Think I'm with you,' Dave said suddenly. 'He set up that — what was it called? — *The Kitty-Cat robbery?*'

'Pussyfoot,' Josh corrected. 'Yeah, a gang callin' themselves the Pussyfooters hit the caravan in the worst place where the wagons couldn't manoeuvre — thanks, of course to Craig — or so it was suspected, but nothin' was ever proved. Army discharged him, anyway. They had to, I guess. Them Pussyfooters got away with thousands. But during the search afterward, every now and again, the army'd come across the body of one of them — no sign of the money, neither.'

'I never heard that before.'

'Yeah, it happened. But there were a few of the Pussyfooters still alive, and they stayed hid — along with the cash.'

Dave said, nodding slowly, 'Recall that none was ever recovered.' Then he snapped his head up. 'Judas! *That's* why Craig was tortured! Someone figured he knew where the loot was — is!'

'Be my guess,' Josh said, and Kel and Hank agreed.

All three were studying Dave as well as they could in the light. He smiled thinly. 'I was a long way from here when all that happened, gents.'

'All right. Rumour has it that what was left of the gang had a falling-out. There was some killing — only a few survived — and the loot was still cached somewhere. Never had many suspects, but one was — '

'Walter P. Craig!' cut in Dave. 'Judas priest! *Has* to be why he was tortured: whoever did it wanted him to tell where the money was hid.'

'That's it, I'd say. Of course 'Craig' wasn't his real name but someone must've recognized him from his old army days, decided to try an' make him spill the beans.'

'Or *did* make him talk,' Dave said quietly.

'There's that,' Josh agreed, sober-faced. 'I guess that's something we'll never know, will we, Mr Brent?'

Dave stiffened. 'Hell! Not you, too! *I* never knew Craig, and wouldn't've recognized him alive or dead. If I had, d'you think I'd be stupid enough to take his name?'

'Mmm — mebbe not,' Josh admitted grudgingly.

'But Barlow or Burns, or both, recognized him, even with his face mangled,' Dave pointed out.

'Yeah, Josh, that's right!' said Kel.

'*How*'d they know him?' asked Hank. 'From dodgers or what?'

'Now that's somethin' to think about!' Josh admitted. 'And damned hard!'

'Case'll send one helluva posse after you,' allowed Kel, talking to Dave, 'if he believes you did know Craig before.'

'Figured that. Why I'm trying to get clear as far and fast as I can.' Dave paused, looked from one to the other. 'Any offers?'

Finally, Hank said, 'Mebbe if you got a deal for us.'

'Got nothing.' They just stared back and he swore. 'Hell! You still don't believe I didn't torture Craig, do you?'

'Well someone who wanted somethin' outa him did,' Josh allowed quietly. 'Wanted it reeaaalll bad.'

'*Not me!* Goddammit, for about the hundredth time *I did not torture Walt Craig!*'

'Then, like you said, you ain't got nothin' to deal with.' Hank looked grim and lifted his shotgun just enough to remind Dave it was still there. 'So you're on your own.'

Dave sighed. 'OK. So what happens? You gonna shoot me? Help me? Hold me for Burns and Barlow?'

'Wouldn't be hard to do that,' Hank said, barely moving his lips, eyes narrowed.

'Not for all of you, mebbe,' Dave admitted, looking hard at the shotgunner. 'But it'd be hard as it ever gets for at least one of you . . . I can guarantee that.'

They were all tense now and maybe there was a hint of real worry starting to show on their faces — Dave was still an unknown quantity, after all.

Hank snorted, but, finally, Josh asked, 'Where you want to go?'

'Anywhere away from here. You choose.'

That surprised them and he saw by the way they exchanged looks that they were finally starting to believe that he really hadn't tortured Craig and so didn't know where the loot was.

And Dave Brent knew that wherever they turned him loose — if they did! — there would be one of them following, night and day, just to make sure.

But he was ready to make a deal, simply because he didn't know of any other way.

For now.

And there was one other thing: how did *these* men know so damned much about Craig and the missing payroll?

7

The River Again!

Dave could sense they didn't want to just turn him loose, which likely meant they weren't quite willing to believe that either he *didn't* torture Craig or whatever his real name was, *or* he got the information he wanted, which in this group's minds could only be the location of the lost army payroll.

They were watching him mighty closely, and Hank's shotgun wandered down to point — casually — in his direction.

'Well, what's it to be, gents?' Dave asked with a rasp in his voice. 'What I've told you is gospel. I'm not after any missing payroll — not that I'm saying I couldn't use the money — but I like money I can spend without worrying that some time a lawman's gonna tap me on the shoulder and stick a gun in my belly when I turn around.'

'Wouldn't have to be a lawman,' commented Kel, and Josh gave him a blistering look.

He stared hard at Dave. 'No reason for us *not* to believe you, I guess, but . . . '

He hesitated and Dave decided to take a chance and get things in the open.

'The first I heard of anyone named Walter P. Craig was when I found his body in the river. Even if I'd known his name before that it wouldn't've meant a damn thing to me. I've got my own problems with the blasted Vandemanns somewhere along my backtrail and that's why I tried to swap identities.'

'Hopin' they'd get to hear that a body had been found carrying papers that identified him as Dave Brent, right?' asked Josh, looking grim, but maybe just a mite uncertain, too. 'I can savvy your thinkin', Dave, but — well, we'd like to be certain sure.'

Hank and Kel murmured something that likely was agreement — and they looked plenty grim.

'I've got no way of proving my story.'

Josh glanced at his pards and then nodded. 'He's right, boys, sounds like he needs a little . . . help!'

Dave was moving before the man had finished speaking, hurling himself headlong, twisting in midair as, startled, they began to scatter.

His gun blazed and he managed to fan off three fast shots before his shoulder hit the ground and jarred through him clear to his toes. He saw Kel and Hank both stumble, trying to dodge his lead. Hank almost dropped the shotgun, but fumbled and caught it again, but not in a position that would allow him to shoot.

Dave saw he was on the edge of a drop and hoped like hell it didn't fall away into any lethal depth as he tumbled over. The shotgun's thunder rang in his ears and a couple of handfuls of dirt erupted ... then he was falling.

He couldn't see properly: the already weak light was almost black wherever he was going right now.

He thought he had snapped his spine as he hit. It must have been a protruding lump of dirt for it crumbled away, turned him so that he almost somersaulted and then his boots were scraping over a sharply angled bank of some kind.

Hell's teeth! It's still deeper! his mind shouted silently. And then he was in space, vaguely aware that guns were being fired above him; one, the second shot from Hank's Greener.

Dave still held his own gun. *Thank you, God! Don't give up on me just yet!*

This last word of his silent prayer was jarred so that he actually said it aloud before he rolled into some brush. He didn't know what kind it was but felt a tingle in his nostrils and closed his eyes instantly — something was getting ready to sting him and he sure didn't want to be blinded right now.

But, although his cheeks and one ear did tingle some his vision wasn't affected, and he kicked away from the brush, landing on hands and knees. The Colt slid from his grip but he dived headlong after it and managed to grab it. Hank had apparently reloaded for the shotgun roared and a basinful of gravel jumped into the air amongst some sparse bushes. He drew up his knees, felt the now exposed cylinder of his gun, ran his finger over the shells — he still had three left.

The trio were shouting above, but their wild shooting drowned out their words. Dave found he had banged his right leg in the fall and it almost folded under him. He went halfway, put down his left hand and made contact with a rock, dragged himself behind it in time to hear the grave-whispering snarl of a bullet that came and went in a burst of sparks. He huddled, decided to shuck out the empty cartridges and thumb in three fresh loads.

With a fully loaded gun in his hand he felt better — not necessarily *safer*, but better.

He heard Josh's voice clearly. 'He can get to the river from here! Kel, this is your territory more'n ours.'

'On my way,' Kel replied.

'Hank, rake the bottom down there.'

'I've only got three more shells, Josh.'

Dave distinctly heard Josh curse. 'And I'm sure Dave will be glad to hear that. You dumb bastard!'

Dave chuckled, thought he heard a murmured 'sorry' from Hank and silently thanked the man — only to have the brush around him erupt as the first blast of buckshot ripped into it. He didn't hesitate. While the echoes were still dying, he lurched up and ran in a series of hopping, humping kind of steps — because of that damn leg! — and hurled himelf into a bigger thicket. Gasping, breath almost battered out of him, he clawed his way into the underbrush, froze, and gritted his teeth as the next blast from Hank whipped overhead. His body wanted to jump and run but he forced himself to lie still, hoping Hank would be reloading and then start shooting elsewhere.

'Come on! Come on!' Josh was yelling, firing down with his six-gun.

Dave moved, hoping their gunfire and the sound of the lead would cover any noise he made. But he didn't move too far, dropped flat, fingers of his free hand clawing into the softish ground. *Not only soft but soggy. Oozing slightly.*

His heart was thudding enough to interfere with his already strained hearing in the wake of another volley of bullets. Then the buckshot once more — Hank must've reloaded at lightning speed! — and he reckoned that was all the ammo Hank had for his weapon. Josh had stopped shooting, and Dave wondered where Kel was.

When he found out a breath later, he almost jumped up in a split second of panic: the man was close! Must've climbed down while the others were shooting. *It took a brave — or stupid — man to do that, the way Josh was riled!*

Then Dave heard through the ringing in his head the unmistakable sound of a pistol chamber being spun as the gunman reloaded. He had to make his move — and fast!

It was a good try, but Kel was faster and Dave felt a wave of true fear wash over him as the man shouted victoriously, 'Got you, Dave! Josh, I've got him! Kill him or . . . what?'

'No!' Dave roared as loud as he could, using the volume of his voice to startle Kel.

It did, and the man gave an involuntary grunt, spun so fast towards the sound that he stumbled — right into the path of the two shots Dave triggered.

The killer collapsed as Josh and Hank both started yelling.

Dave plunged away, his injured leg hurting and even slowing him, but he had heard something through the disorienting noises in his head from all the shooting.

The distinctive, unmistakable sound of running water. He had been almost on the river-bank and hadn't realizd it.

They were shooting again and he heard lead tearing through the brush — then one or two *zipped* into the river ahead.

He veered, but only slightly, plunged into the shallows and immediately felt the tug of a current — not a really powerful one, but at least it told him which way the river was flowing, and it was in the direction he wanted to go — away from his pursuers.

He rammed his gun into his waistband inside his shirt: it was the only weapon he had right now and he didn't want to lose it. True, he carried a hunting knife on his belt, but figured he wouldn't get close enough to the hunters to use it. Not that he wanted to; he had been in knife fights and he hadn't enjoyed any of them, even though he had walked or crawled away as the winner.

Now the river had him and he gasped at the coldness of the water, thought he heard a shout, and then there were a couple of splashes to his left that could have been made by bullets.

He had no control of direction, so just relaxed bunched muscles and allowed the river to carry him where it would. What he could see of the world blurred by . . .

The current drove him with considerable force under a cutbank and his head rang and buzzed as it contacted the overhang, a mixture of tree roots, partly exposed rocks and water-compacted earth. He got a hold with aching fingers.

For now, he was more than ready to call this hole *home*.

⋆ ⋆ ⋆

They didn't give up easily.

Not that he expected they would, but

they damn near wore him down to where he made mistakes that could get him killed.

He was already cold from hanging in the water for so long, caught an occasional glimpse of them moving along the opposite bank. Every so often, one of them would squat and squint, or even lie down on his belly, in an effort to see under the overhanging bank on this side — where, of course, Dave was.

He tried not to move and break the flow of current — these were outdoorsmen, ex-army, he suspected, and they would know to look for such signs. He didn't know how much longer it was before he saw one of them — Hank, he thought — wading into the river — *No!* Wading *across*, holding a long sapling with a splintery end over his head.

Dave knew what that meant — he was aiming to probe beneath the overhangs, poke and jab with the splintered end of the sapling and hope to make contact.

These were a bunch of mean bastards, all right!

He tried to worm his way back but he was about as far under as he could go, hunched down now he had moved right up into the rear of his hideaway. He cringed unconsciously as he felt the stomping of another searcher above, and a voice yelled, 'Here, Hank! Feels like a space under here! Mebbe I can jump hard enough to break away the overhang.'

'Damn fool! If he's there he'll kill you soon as it gives way. I'll take a few jabs and we'll soon see.' He laughed briefly. 'If it comes out bloody, we'll know he's there.'

The man didn't answer but the jumping up and down stopped — and then Dave almost yelled as the probing sapling rammed past his wet face and gouged into the mud where his head rested. He submerged, holding a quick breath, as the splintery end was withdrawn a few inches, moved slightly and then rammed forward again with maiming force. It took his hat off, mashed it back into the mud and he grabbed it swiftly.

'Hey! I think I got somethin'!'

Dave eased his mouth above the muddy water as the sapling withdrew for its next probe, gulped down as much air as he could and sank under. His hands clawed at the muddy bottom but it was too soft for a decent hold. He felt the water disturbed by the stabbing sapling, lifted an arm and actually deflected it, swallowing a yelp of agony as a long splinter broke off in his forearm.

Hell! His lungs were bursting and that damn probe kept jabbing and stabbing, coming closer to his body. If it touched him, the man using it would know immediately and he would be a goner.

He fended it off one more time and figured he would have to come up for air, when suddenly it was withdrawn. He shoved his face into the few inches of air between the surface of the muddy water and wet soil of the overhang, trying to stifle his gulping, retching sounds.

But the searcher yelled, 'Ah! He ain't here. Must've washed further down. The current's pretty strong.'

'Well, get lookin', dammit!' bawled Josh.

Dave clung there to an overhead root, fingers skinned and stinging, fighting the urge to be sick — this river's water was not the sweetest he'd ever swallowed!

He went into a kind of half-trance, hanging on, aware of where he was, but his mind swirling so that every so often he gave a start and convulsively tightened his grip on the protruding root to keep from passing out entirely.

He thought he could hear distant shouting intermittently. He was stiff with cold, teeth beginning to chatter. He hoped it wouldn't be loud enough for anyone outside to hear. *Crazy, amigo! You'd knock your teeth out of your gums if it was that loud!*

He murmured as if half asleep, the cold working up into his brain. Then one time when he jolted awake with a convulsive jerk, he realized he could now see the actual root he clung to poking through the overhang's soil!

'Godamighty,' he breathed. 'Almost daylight.'

Now the search would be that much easier for *them* and that much more dangerous for him.

8

Ride or Run

Cautiously, clamping his jaws and aching teeth, Dave went hand-over-hand towards the opening. It was only a few feet in reality, but it felt like half a mile, his cramped and burning arm muscles straining, legs clumsy.

His breath rattled like a Gatling gun with a feed stoppage. He plunged his face under and gasped, shaking water from his hair as he emerged into the river itself. Almost immediately he swung back, just far enough to duck under the overhang.

But he need not have worried: looking out like a hiding cat who is not sure if he's in trouble with his master, he scanned the opposite bank as far as he could see to the right, then did the same to the left.

No one!

He paused as he instinctively started to show himself, but thought, *What the hell! I've got to get going or I'll cramp up with the damn c-c-c-cold . . .*

He took one more long look, decided he hadn't made a mistake, that there was no other human being anywhere in sight.

So he turned face-in towards the bank and used his aching arms to steady himself as he started upstream.

It had to be that way: through the ringing and other strange noises in his head, he recalled hearing Hank call to Josh that he figured Dave had been carried downstream by the current. Leastways, he *thought* that's what he had heard. The hell with it. He only had the two choices — up or down — and he was sure Hank and Josh had decided to look downstream.

God knew how much time had passed since he had heard those words, but it hadn't been light enough to see more than grey images then. Now there were patches of pale-gold sunlight dappling the river and its banks.

Time to make a decision and *move*, Goddammit!

So he moved. Allowed the moderate current to carry him a few yards, and then, his boots barely touching the soft bottom, he lunged for the bank, grabbed the base of a small, overhanging bush, and hauled himself out onto the grass.

Gasping and floundering like a newly landed fish, only not so energetically, he rolled onto his back, stayed there long enough to gulp several lungfuls of air, then twisted onto his side and clawed his way upright.

Hell! His legs were shaking like he'd run a mile in ankle chains.

He swayed and steadied himself against a sapling, head hanging as he stomped his feet, feeling the blood beginning to sing through his veins again.

A glance at the sky gave him a surge of energy, enough to get moving away from the water's edge, and into the screening bush and light timber.

He figured he had only gone about ten or twelve yards when he smelled smoke.

His first panicky thought was they had set fire to the brush, but his senses detected a hint of — *bacon*, for God's sake . . .

It must be someone's breakfast fire.

Instantly his stomach started growling with hunger and he sniffed the air several times, picked a direction he thought was correct, and started working his way through chest-high scrub, pausing occasionally to make sure he was still on track.

The smell of cooking was strong and he was salivating, when a sobering thought struck him.

His gun! It had been submerged in water for hours and so had his bullet belt.

There was a mighty good chance that the weapon was waterlogged and wouldn't fire, or the indifferent cartridges that were often shipped out to the frontier lands by unscrupulous town dealers could be reject seconds and far from reliable.

He had to get a look at this fire and who was doing the cooking. It wasn't likely that it was Josh and Hank: they had enough savvy not to do such a foolish thing under the circumstances. A greenhorn, then, someone convinced he was starving and who had decided to cook bacon before he succumbed.

Hell! The notion spun around inside his head and he wished his tobacco was dry; a calming cigarette smoked leisurely would have been more than welcome.

'Who the hell're you?'

Dave spun, going down into the gunfighter's crouch instinctively and palming up the suspect Colt. He glimpsed a darkish form, shadowed by a thickly leaved bush.

The man gasped and stepped back, white-faced and off-balance briefly. When he steadied again, Dave had his left hand on the muzzle of the carbine the man held and was thrusting it away to one side as he brought up the Colt in his right hand, cocking the hammer.

There was no way the stranger could know it might not shoot.

'*Hey! Hey! Wait!*' the man shouted, backing off another step, releasing his hold on the carbine. 'Don't — don't shoot! I-I dunno you . . . '

'Never seen you before, neither,' Dave told him flatly, squinting. He ran his gaze over the other's rumpled and slightly torn frock coat, his soiled shirt front, dishevelled hair — and scratched face. Under the dirt and dried blood Dave reckoned he was young — early twenties, no more. He still held the carbine but then let it fall.

'You're who?' Dave snapped, and the younger man blinked, looking really worried now as he tried to back up a little more, his eyes on the carbine in the grass. He was cramped by the thicket and Dave caught a glimpse of a small camp-fire through the leaves, a skillet sitting precariously on a few uneven stones, bacon sizzling.

'Tell you what,' Dave said, nodding towards the thicket. 'Let's talk about names over a slice or two of that there bacon. I'll even tell you mine now — Dave Brent — and, if I'm not mistaken, you'd be ... Morg Longstreet?'

'How-how'd you know that?'

'Relax, Morg, I've got no argument with you, but I do have with the same men lookin' for you: Josh and Hank. Don't worry about Kel. I think I either killed or winged him. Either way I think he's out of it for now.'

The young fugitive stared at Dave, ran a tongue around obviously dry lips. 'How you know they're huntin' me?'

'Few things they said. Like your relationship with Josh's wife.'

Morg seemed to sag in on himself a little. 'It ain't true! We used to go to school together and ... aw, well, we did get together once. It was accidental, our meetin', I mean. She was bathing in the river and I'd just had a ducking when my hoss throwed me and had stripped down to ... well, I was almost bare-assed an' — ' He shrugged.

'An' nature took its course. Be temptin', I guess.'

Morg smiled tentatively at Dave. 'That-that's what I tried to explain! But that damn Josh, he slapped Bridget — that's her name — and then started in on me, but I tripped him somehow, or he fell chasin' me. In any case I got away, but them pards of his were handy and — well, Judas! They got me on the run now and-and I'm hardly game to close my eyes ... I swear. I ain't been sparkin' Bridget like he claims.' He went silent and swallowed, adding sheepishly, 'Trouble is, I got a bit of a name as a ... womanizer. But it's only with them silly young things who work in Bixby and ... they like bein' kinda teased an' — '

'Morg, you're a damn fool in lots of ways, it seems, but lighting a cooking fire with those sonuvers after you ... ' Dave shook his head. 'Plumb loco, boy!

But I'm screamin' hungry, so let's talk about it over some of that sowbelly.'

'S-sure. I-I thought I'd shook 'em an' I was starvin'.' He was eager, now, sounded relieved, happy to have some company. He admitted it was stupid lighting the fire, but he had seen Josh and Hank on the far bank, way downstream, and the wind was blowing *from* them and he was *hungry*, like only a young man could be with food in his saddle-bags and ready to take a chance he wouldn't give away his position.

'Still damn risky, boy,' Dave told him, chomping on some bacon and savouring it. 'But you cook pretty good, or it's just that I'm so damn hungry I'd risk takin' a freshly killed rabbit out of the jaws of a cougar.'

Morg Longstreet grinned around his mouthful of food, a reckless, good-looking young man, forgetting his troubles for the moment.

'You afoot?'

Morg looked doubtful. 'Well, kind of. They scared off my horse but this big black wandered into my camp a couple hours ago, saddled an' all, and he seemed friendly, even let me ride him for a couple miles. When I figured I was far enough away from where Josh was searchin', I stopped to make my fire, found a grubsack in the saddle-bags and — well, by the time I cooked this here bacon, the black had wandered off. Couldn't've gone far. I — What's wrong? Why you sort of half-smiling?'

'Morg, we're eating *my* bacon. That horse is mine and I'd sure like to be straddling him right now. Where'd he go?'

Morg started to get to his feet, looking off into the trees. 'I — well, I thought he was just over there, munchin' on a patch of grass. I was gonna ease the cinchstrap and make things a mite more comfortable for him.'

'He's likely looking for me.'

Dave heaved to his feet, glancing anxiously in the direction Longstreet had pointed. 'Too bad you never thought to ground-hitch him,' he said curtly, pursed his lips to whistle, but paused. The morning was quite still and the sound might alert Josh and the others: he wasn't certain just how close they might be and —

Then his belly knotted as a voice bellowed from the timber not far downstream.

'Well, looky here, Dave, ol' *compadre*! I got me a really fine-lookin' black horse. White tip on one ear, roughly shaped star on his chest. Man, I b'lieve this might be yours!'

Morg gulped, looking guiltily at the grim-faced Dave. 'I-I'm real sorry, Dave! Honest! I-I — '

Dave held up a hand as Josh's voice reached them again.

'Tell you what, Dave, you want this fine-looking bronc, you come an' get him. I figure you ain't too far away, and you can hear me. I hope you can, 'cause I'm only gonna give you a few minutes to show yourself or call out an' then I'm gonna kill this here black!'

'Oh, Jesus, what've I done?' murmured Morg, looking sick. 'Dave, I — '

Dave, white-faced now, held up a hand. Beads of sweat popped out on his face as he heard the unmistakable whinny of the black. His hands knotted down at his sides.

He jumped when a gun fired. Morg looked sick.

Josh's laugh came clearly. 'Bet that made you sit up, eh, *amigo*? See, I changed my mind. Oh, I still aim to kill the bronc, but I thought, why make it quick? Why not shoot a bit here, another bit there — make him whinny an' whine — loud enough to bring you to me with your hands in the air, of course. I'll give you — aw, yeah, I feel kinda generous. I'll give you five shots — give the *hoss* five shots, I mean. But you know that, don't you? Reckon I can do it an' keep him alive for a while — kind of! — till you get here. Then you can watch me act real humane while I give him that last shot that'll put him outa his misery. You *hope*. How's that for a deal? Interested?'

Dave's legs turned to water when Josh's words were followed by the sound of a gun firing and a shrill cry came from the black horse.

There was a pause, the echoes of the gunshot drifting away through the timber, followed by Josh's voice.

'That's one! Jeez, blood sure stands out agin the black hide an' that chest blaze! Number two comin' up, Dave.'

'Hold it, you son of a bitch!' Dave yelled. 'I'm comin' to you. Don't hurt him any more — you do, I'll kill you with a gutshot!'

Josh laughed. 'Come on in, Dave. Be glad to see you.'

Morg Longstreet backed away from the look on Dave's face. 'I-I din' mean . . . '

'Quit it, Morg, it's not your fault. But I guess you know how mean this sonuver can be.'

'Who, Josh Keeler?'

'Whatever his name is. Seems to like

hunting people and defenceless women and horses.'

Morg cleared his throat. 'L-look, Dave, he ain't really huntin' me for messin' with his wife, that's just a cover-up.'

Dave frowned, tense as a gallows rope stretched with its victim's weight. 'For what?'

Morg Longstreet released a gusting breath. They both jumped at the sound of another shot.

'Hey, Dave! Just in case you think I'm foolin'. That was only a close one, gettin' the black all on edge. Next one goes through his right shoulder 'less I see you in about ten seconds!'

Dave grabbed the startled Morg and threw him through the screening scrub. He yelled and stumbled to his knees and Josh fired. Longstreet yelled, jerked and rolled, clawing at a blood-flecked shot high on his right arm. *Just a scratch.*

'Ah, Dave, you smart-ass son-of-a-*bitch*! Was lookin' forward to puttin' a couple into you, kinda matchin' shot-for-shot — one for the black, one for you. You done spoiled things for me, but that damn Morg is gonna make a good target, long an' skinny though he is!'

He fired again, but Morg was lunging back and Dave reached out, dragged him into the brush and heaved him away as far as he could, hurling himself in the other direction.

A carbine opened up as well as the six-gun, raking the thicket, the bullets rattling as they snarled through drying twigs, scattering leaves. *That would be Hank.*

'By God, Dave, I'm sure gonna enjoy nailin' you! Mebbe this'll hurry you up!'

'*Don't shoot!*' Dave yelled. 'Don't touch that horse, Josh, I'm comin' out.'

'You better have your hands in the air.'

'They're already up. Here I come.'

'You're crazy!' Morg hissed, breathless, eyes wide and staring. 'He'll kill you!'

'No he won't. He needs to do some more gloating. Anyway, you're gonna be my stand-in again. Dive low!'

'Hey! No! Aw, hell . . . '

Morg was backing off but Dave grabbed his shirt front and sent him staggering into the open.

There were two shots as Morg sprawled headlong and Dave lunged away through the brush, charging in the direction of Josh's voice. The killer wasn't prepared for that and Hank's voice, high-pitched with tension and surprise, yelled, 'Jesus Christ, he's comin'! I'm goin' — '

Dave burst through a screen of brush, using his left arm across his face to shield his eyes, dropping it the moment he had cleared the raking branches. He glimpsed Josh and Hank both starting to run for thicker cover and he propped, pulling the trigger of his Colt.

To his surprise it fired, although the sound was more of a *splat!* than a roar. Josh stumbled, grabbing at his right shoulder, blinked in surprise when he realized the bullet striking was no worse than a stone from a kid's slingshot.

He grinned crookedly. 'Well! Havin' trouble with your ammo, Dave?'

'He may be, but I ain't!'

Morg's voice was close enough behind Dave to make him whirl in genuine surprise, even as Morg cut loose with two fast shots. They passed close to Josh, and Hank was already stumbling away. Both killers rushed into the brush as Dave triggered again. This time the gun didn't fire, but the sound of the hammer falling on a cold chamber was covered by the blast of Morg's pistol.

They kept running and by then Dave was lunging into the brush where the black was whinnying, reins looped over a low branch. It wrenched its head wildly, eyes rolling, as Dave knocked the reins loose, held them taut, then slid his hand up to the frightened animal's head and started talking in a quiet voice as he rubbed its ear, the one with the white tip.

The horse was still skittish, had obviously been frightened by Josh's pistol, although Dave couldn't see any wound — there was no blood staining the chest blaze as Josh had inferred. Not that he thought the man had any real concern for the horse's welfare — more likely he realized he could ask a high price for such a mount as this, but only if it was unharmed.

'Hell! You-you left me out there! You *threw* me at him!' gasped Morg with rising anger. 'Dammit! I-I *helped* you an' you-you damn well went to that horse first!'

'He's my friend, Morg,' Dave told him, deadpan. 'Mebbe when I get to know you better, I'll give you priority.'

'You can stick that — whatever the hell it is! *Jeez!* I can't believe you *done* that!'

Dave shrugged, unrepentant, stroking and calming the black now as it nuzzled him in welcome.

'He can carry us both outa here,'

Dave said. 'But how about this — Bridget, was it? She be safe from Josh?'

Morg Longstreet's face was still stony but he calmed down quickly enough now, blood draining from his face.

He startled Dave when he said, 'Josh ain't really after me for romancin' Bridget.'

'Well, what the hell is he tryin' to kill you for?'

''Cause I seen him and Hank Ivey and Kel Raines torturin' that feller you found floatin' in the river — Walt Craig. *That*'s why he wants to kill me. I'm the only witness.'

9

Witness

'*You saw what they did to Walt Craig?*'

Dave stared hard at the youth. There was no reason why he should lie — none that Dave could think of, anyway — but it was a break Dave, at least, hadn't expected.

Morg Longstreet nodded, his mouth drawn a little tight. 'Yeah. I'd been runnin' and lost my horse, could hear Josh and them searchin' for me and I *knew* that they'd kill me if they caught me.' He looked sheepish as he added, 'I-I guess you'd say I panicked.'

'No shame in that, boy, not with a pair of mean bastards like them spurrin' you on.'

Morg just nodded: it was obvious his thoughts were right back in that time now and it had shaken him considerably. 'Well, I fell in the damn river again. I can swim all right and thought OK, let 'em search on land, see if I can get away by floatin' and swimmin' downstream.'

It had exhausted him sooner than he had hoped and, panting and gasping, he made his way to shore, dragged himself up and flopped under some brush. He passed out for a time, awoke to the sounds of mean, shouting voices and —

'A scream to turn your blood cold, Dave.' His voice shook at the memory and his face was pale and blotchy again. His hands were clenching and unclenching but Dave figured Morg wasn't even aware of this, still overwhelmed by the memory of what he had heard and seen.

'They had him on his knees, tied to a tree. His face — well, it wasn't much of a face any more, all blood and his nose was broke and mashed back, his mouth just a-a mess!' He blew out his cheeks. 'I still feel queasy just recollectin'.'

'Take your time, boy,' Dave said grimly. 'I saw that face — or what was left of it. Thought it'd been done by the rapids Craig was washed over.'

'M-might've sort of finished things off, but mostly it was done by Josh smashing Craig's face into the tree: it had rough bark.' He had to stop, clamped a hand over his mouth and writhed a little, but didn't vomit, although Dave figured it must've taken quite an effort not to.

'They were both kickin' Craig and I heard his ribs crack once.'

'Christ! How'd they expect him to tell them anything if they were beating him to death?'

'Nearly, anyway, but then Josh took a cheroot and lit it and began burnin' him. Even ripped his trousers down an' — '

'I get the picture, Morg. How long did this go on for?'

'I dunno. I wasn't game to move. I just stayed put, couldn't . . . couldn't take my eyes off what they were doin'.

Then Josh seemed to . . . well, he nearly had a fit, I reckon. He grabbed poor Craig by the throat and started shoutin' into that bloody mess that was his face: '*What'd you do with it? You lousy double-crossin' bastard! What did you do with it? Where'd you hide it?*' He calmed down a little when Hank grabbed his arm and said he'd kill Craig before he could tell them where he'd hid the payroll if he wasn't careful.'

Dave nodded. 'Yeah, I've finally worked out that Craig must've been the pathfinder for those army pay deliveries. He faked a raid, probably killed off the escort, or left 'em to die in the desert. Likely hid the money, and then showed up all busted-up and exhausted from a walk across the salt pans. A hero.' Dave looked at Morg. 'No need to tell me any more, Morg, they went too far, killed Craig with their beating and torture.'

Morg nodded, still clenching one hand. 'I thought Josh was gonna murder Hank: he blamed him for killin' Craig. Then they realized they had to get rid of the body. I wanted to clear out, but stayed put, climbed a tree when they took Craig away, seen 'em dump him in the river, poke him with sticks to get him out into the current that'd carry him over the rapids and the rocks.'

'Could've worked, too, except that undertaker in Bixby did his job too well and noticed all the torture wounds on Craig.'

'I seen you come in later an' find him but when them kids brought Burns back after the body'd washed down among 'em, I just lit out.'

'How'd Josh and Hank know you'd seen what they'd done?'

'Seen me running off, I guess. I was scared and careless, too. Took a tumble down a steep slope that almost rolled me into their camp. They knew where I must've come from, slidin' down from that direction. I-I been runnin' ever since.'

'Why didn't you go to Burns? Or old Case Barlow himself? Tell 'em what you'd seen?'

Dave was puzzled when Morg Longstreet looked at him kind of strange and smiled twistedly.

'Didn't I tell you? At one stage when they were takin' a breather and givin' Craig time to come round, Hank said, 'Lew an' Case won't be too happy when they see the mess we've made of Craig.' And Josh looked real mean and spoke with his teeth clenched. 'We'll throw him over the rapids and let them rocks mess him up some more, *and* — just between you an' me, Lew Burns and damn Case Barlow *don't need to know if we got anythin' outa Craig! Savvy?*'

'Well, I swear Hank's jaw dropped to his belly button he was so took-back. 'You *savvy?*' Josh said again, through his teeth. '*They don't need to know nothin'*. We were after Craig and he slipped into the river, got carried over the rapids — our bad luck it killed him before we could get him to tell where the payroll was.' Jeez, Dave, I was sure they'd hear my teeth rattlin' an' I just went to ground until I took that tumble down the slope.'

'How'd you get away?'

'Ran! Judas priest, I never knew I could run so fast and — well, I did know that country pretty well: used to play hooky up there instead of goin to school sometimes an' . . . an' . . . ' He almost blushed as he added, 'That's where I got my reputation for bein' a bit of a ladies' man, too.'

Dave grinned. 'You've led an interesting life, kid. Me, my old man wore me out behind a plough or swingin' an axe or diggin' fence-post holes and so on, never had any spare energy for chasing girls at your age.'

Morg nodded, then looked sideways at Dave. 'But you made up for lost time, I bet. When you left home, I mean?'

'Let's just say I've had my moments with the ladies. Now I think it's time we lit out and left Josh and Hank — *and them* crooked lawmen — to . . . whatever they want to get up to.'

'I guess.'

'You sound disappointed, kid.'

'Well, I was thinking; you know how to handle yourself, we could kinda throw in together, couldn't we?'

'For what?' Dave kept his voice level, his face blank.

'Aw, come on! You know what I'm gettin' at.'

'No, I don't, Morg, but if you want to spell it out, first think of this: there's nothing you can do about recovering that payroll because you don't know where it is. Getting a share of that *is* what you had in mind, ain't it?'

'Well, yeah. Mebbe just sharin' a reward for findin' it . . . ?'

Dave smiled crookedly. 'Good thinkin'. But same thing applies, kid: *you gotta find it first.*'

Morg grinned widely, smacked the heel of a hand against his forehead.

'There's somethin' else I oughta tell you, too, Dave.'

Dave felt his breath still for a moment. 'Tell me what?'

'I know where that payroll money is hid.'

He went silent as Dave stared back at him, obviously sceptical.

'And how would *you* know the hiding place, Morg?' he asked quietly. 'Craig didn't tell them — just misled 'em.'

The kid grinned and shook a finger in Dave's direction. 'Don't be too sure I'm talkin' through my hat, Dave!'

Dave heaved a sigh and nodded slowly. 'Got to be a habit over the years, takin' nothin' for granted unless I could see it or feel it. But, go on, kid, I'm listenin'.'

'I'll bet you are!' Morg was quite smug now and Dave had the feeling that whatever Morgan Longstreet had to say next was going to be worth listening to.

It went back to the girl — Bridget.

Josh had done a deal with Bridget's

father — he badly wanted a stud bull Old Man Gerholdt had won in a poker game and didn't know what to do with. And he wanted to get rid of Bridget, too. Seems they did nothing but fight.

But while he maybe was an easy victim when the cards were shuffled in everyone's favour but his, Old Hans was a canny type, could sense money in all its shapes and forms.

So when Josh Keeler, an arrogant small-time rancher on his way to becoming an arrogant *big*-time rancher at any cost other than his, made a paltry offer for the bull, he sensed the animal was being way, way undervalued.

His thick Teutonic accent had never been thicker than when he came to dicker over price. He made sure the less than amiable Keeler couldn't understand much of what he said, but did a lot of arm-waving, lifting and lowering of his voice. But Josh Keeler didn't aim to be outsmarted by some squarehead who couldn't even speak American fluently.

Tight with a dollar, Josh was close to giving up and forgetting the bull, when he saw Bridget, just a glimpse through carefully parted drapes at the window of her bedroom. Not one to miss a trick, and appearing most uninterested, Gerholdt filed away that lusting look on Josh's face and next day he sealed the bargain.

He would accept Josh Keeler's monetary offer for the bull — although he made it perfectly clear that he thought it was too low — but only on the condition that Josh married Bridget, who at seventeen or eighteen was becoming a worry and a financial burden to her father — not that Hans mentioned that Keeler agreed — then the bull was his.

Josh fell for it and rode home with the bull *and* a new wife. He was intensely jealous and more than one amorous cowhand lost some teeth and learned what it was like to have a broken nose or arm before a few weeks had passed.

Josh caught her with Morg Longstreet on the riverbank and if the girl hadn't tripped him would have shot the boy dead on the spot. He slapped the girl about very roughly, so much so that her father sobered up long enough to come over with his ancient Bavarian shotgun and demand that Keeler pay his daughter's medical bills or . . . he lifted the heavy old shotgun threateningly.

Threateningly enough for Josh Keeler to get off with not much more than a reprimand from the lecherous old judge for defending himself against Hans Gerholdt.

Bridget had had little feeling for her drunken father but she did try to poison Josh's coffee and when he realized it he took a whip to her and she fled. It was never proven for sure, but someone — perhaps Morg Longstreet — helped the girl get away one night and she took off and ended up almost dying of thirst and hunger in the Great Salty — the Big Tablecloth — many miles to the south.

Josh dragged her back to the ranch and warned her that next time he would flay the hide off Morg Longstreet while she watched, and then he would start on her.

'Hard bastard,' Dave allowed, when Morg had finally finished his tale. 'But what's all this got to do with you knowing where the army payroll is stashed?'

Morg smiled slowly, eyes twinkling. 'That's somethin' that I know and you don't, ain't it?'

'Well, are you gonna tell me or not?'

'Mmm. Yeah, think I will. But hang on to your hat.'

Despite Morg's attempt at a big build-up, there wasn't much to tell at all. Still, what there was packed a considerable wallop.

The girl was smarter than she made out.

When she ran, she ran to the railway line where it reached Scalplock Bend, a steep, winding rise where the train slowed to walking pace. She swung aboard a boxcar — there was a bearded old drifter already there but no details about anything that went on inside.

But when the train skirted the edge of the salt drift, Bridget either jumped or was thrown off. She landed without serious injury, clambered her way up a hill and, exhausted, flopped down in the shade of a boulder on top. She dozed, half-heard voices on the other side of the boulder, and opened her eyes.

'There were three men digging on the side of the hill,' Morg said. 'She recognized one who had come to her father's ranch looking to buy a packhorse.' The boy gave the impatient Dave a crooked smile. 'It was Walt Craig.'

He paused, but Dave gestured for him to continue.

'Well, those fellers were now fillin' in and coverin' up whatever they'd buried. Then, while they were takin' a breather and rollin' cigarettes, Walt Craig up and shot the other two dead. He tipped the bodies into the hole and filled it in.' He paused again, shrugged. 'Bridget hid out till he was gone and — well, she got picked up by a mule-train makin' for the lumber camp at Medicine Bow but someone recognized her and took her back to Josh and . . . and that's it. What them fellers buried *had* to be the army payroll, didn't it, Dave?'

'It's a good chance it was, I guess. Nothing certain, though, Morg,' Dave told him cautiously.

'It is for me!' Morg said stubbornly. 'What else would make 'em dig in the heat of that salt pan?'

'Good point. Thing is, Morg, can you find that place?'

Morg Longstreet's face sobered noticeably. 'Well, I reckon so. Bridget gave me some landmarks. Come on, Dave! You know it's gotta be the payroll! All we have to do is go get it.'

'Yeah,' Dave agreed heavily. '*That's all.*'

10

Pay Day

Sheriff Case Barlow looked up irritably from the papers he was reading as the door of his office opened. He blinked and set the papers aside at once.

Lew Burns was coming through the doorway, using a cane, dragging his left leg a little. His head had a bandage showing beneath his hat and his swollen, bruised face sported two short lengths of tape covering places where wounds had been sutured. His left eye was almost completely closed.

He limped to a chair near the sheriff's desk and practically fell into it.

'You look like hell, Lew,' Barlow grated. 'What're you doing here? Thought you were in the infirmary.'

Burns was breathing fairly heavily and he grimaced a few times, shaking his head . . . carefully.

'No time for me to be out of action, Case.' His voice was weaker, huskier than usual and his swollen mouth seemed to hurt him when he spoke. 'I walked out — *limped* out.'

'Hell, din' expect you to come back on duty after the way that sonofabitch beat up on you. Fact, I'd rather you'd stayed abed for a spell. Get well enough so you can really help when I need you.'

Those blackened eyes looked steadily at Barlow. 'Yeah, well, I figured to be on hand at that time, too.' He paused but Barlow's face was without expression. 'That damn Brent near killed me an' I aim to — to return him the favour.'

'Not in the shape you're in. Hell, Lew, you must've gotten him mighty riled for him to do you like he done.'

Burns curled a lip, winced when the skin split a little and a bead of blood appeared at the corner of his lopsided mouth. 'Underestimated the sonuver! He's one tough *hombre*, Case. We've gotta go careful or he'll kill both of us.'

'The hell he will!' Barlow slapped a hand briefly against his gun butt. 'I ain't gonna waste words on him when we meet. He'll do *just* like I say or I'll shoot him where he stands and think up a reason afterwards.'

'I'm all for that! You know if Morg Longstreet's still sidin' him?'

'Dunno about *sidin'* him but far as I know he's still with him. Lew, you really do look bad. I'm not trying to make you feel worse but — '

'Doubt that you could, Case. No, I gotta do this. Hell, I can't let Brent get away with messin' me up like this. I'll never get anyone to respect me. I gotta get out there and find him and mark him up good — or *bad*, which is better. I gotta show folk I ain't gonna let him get away with it.'

'Well, I admire your spunk, Lew. Must take a deal of willpower and effort, but, thing is, I dunno where the hell he is. Had men out lookin' all over and best I can come up with he's got the Longstreet kid with him and you know what a pain in the ass he can be, kid or not.'

'What about that Gerholdt gal? She likely knows somethin'.'

Barlow showed interest. 'Now that's a thought, but Josh Keeler's been houndin' the hell outa her — she is his wife, after all — but she might give him the slip.'

'*Kind of* his wife,' Burns corrected him. 'I mean, her old man was s'posed to've married 'em, but he ain't no real parson. I don't reckon that marriage'd be recognized.'

'Hell, I don't care one way or t'other. But you're right: she might be the one to lead us to Brent.'

Burns managed a grin this time. 'And he *is* an escaped prisoner. A little shootin' on our part could be quite legal, huh, Case?'

Unsmiling, Barlow nodded jerkily.

'Damn legal. But I got me a queer feelin' about that Brent. I-I dunno just how to put it, but I reckon he's the one gonna lead us to that payroll somehow or other.'

Burns arched his eyebrows and winced when one of the sutures in a cut above his left eye popped and a little blood trickled. 'God-*damn*! But that *stings*! Judas! Well, I gotta say I dunno how he's gonna do that, Case, but if you're serious, then let's go drag the sonuver in.'

'Told you I dunno where he is. Got men still lookin', but no luck yet. Might be best to just let him lead us.'

'Hell, we was just talking about the girl: find her, we'll find him, I reckon.'

Barlow liked the idea.

'Go see Josh — He's got all kindsa friends right through the county. And most folk jump when he says to jump 'cause he's mean as a cross-eyed rattler when he wants to be.'

'An' he's sure achin' to get Brent in his sights. Lew, glad you dragged yourself down here after all! I'll get some of the boys lookin' out specially to help Josh. With any luck we'll have us a lead to Brent by sundown.'

Burns hauled to his feet with a series of grunts, sort of hopped around his walking stick and leaned on it, squarely facing across the desk now.

'Just one thing, Case, leave him just a leetle bit alive for me. OK?'

Case Barlow nodded, a slight twitch at the corners of his hard mouth. 'Pleasure, Lew! A re-e-alll pleasure.'

★ ★ ★

'This here is Bridget, Dave.'

Dave Brent looked at the girl standing beside Morg Longstreet, somewhat surprised. She looked like a schoolgirl — well, until you took a moment to study those knowing grey eyes a little. They seemed to drill right into you, moving slightly in their sockets as she took in every visible part of whoever was facing her.

Morg was a tall streak of misery, 'gangling' likely best described him, and this made her look smaller than she was. Small, yes, but she was a full-grown woman, there could be no mistaking that. Her figure was in proportion to her stature and, Dave admitted silently, it was mighty pleasant to see.

She had a mop of naturally wavy dark hair, somewhere between brown and black, a hard colour to pin a name on. And it framed a 'nice' face: he couldn't think of another word that fitted better, but anyone with a real interest could see it was a face that had experienced many things, well beyond most girls of her years. But her carriage told him she had met and squarely faced each one, the good and the bad, and — well, the thought slid into his head: '*What you see is what you get.*' That would be her attitude.

He caught movement out of the corner of his right eye and glanced down, saw that she was offering him a small hand, with work-worn nails, a little ragged skin around them, but mostly clean.

'How are you, Dave?' Her voice was

firm, easy, not strained, and those eyes looked up squarely into his face.

'Reckon I'm not too bad,' he said, smiling slightly as he took her hand and felt its firmness — and the work callouses that hadn't been visible before. 'Bridget, is it?'

She nodded. 'Sometimes Bridie, but if I'm in a bad mood I won't answer to that.'

'Don't blame you. I've got the same sort of thing about Davey-boy.'

'Oh, no!' she said, shaking her head. 'You don't look like a Davey-boy to me — nor David. It has to be Dave.'

'Well, we're agreed on something . . . '

'Glad to hear that!' Morg said with a smile, adding, when the girl looked at him sharply, 'Oh? You remember me? I'm the feller sittin' here waitin' for you and Dave to decide which name is gonna suit you best. You ask me — '

She laughed briefly, punched him lightly on the arm. 'How could I forget a long streak of misery like you?'

'Not possible,' he countered, adding, 'Shorty.'

Dave stood there and watched and listened to their good-natured banter. He hadn't expected anything like this. Somehow after hearing about what the girl had been through, especially the whipping by Josh Keeler, he had expected something a touch more serious, or at least more subdued.

But he liked it this way better: people who could put an ugly experience behind them so easily usually had few problems they couldn't handle.

When he glanced down he was surprised to see her studying him quite seriously, those eyes seeming to see right inside him.

'What'd I do?' he asked quietly, and it took several long seconds before she blinked and said, 'Wha — ?' She looked puzzled and he touched his face near his own eyes. 'Oh!' She gave a small start. 'I'm sorry! It's a habit of mine. I like to fill my mind with a picture of someone I've just met — if I find them interesting, of course — and take it away with me, go over it in my head at my leisure. It's not very polite, I suppose, but' — she shrugged her small shoulders — 'it's just me.'

'Keep it that way. Sounds like a good idea.'

She smiled and there was a kind of soft light that touched her eyes as the skin crinkled around them.

'I think I'll take your advice.' She turned to Morg. 'We'd best leave tonight. Someone's probably watching us right now, but if we can get horses without making it too obvious, I think it would be best to leave around midnight — the moon doesn't rise till well towards morning.'

'OK by me. You, Dave?'

'Yeah, but how about moving the money? Will we need a buckboard, or something?'

'It's not in crates or chests!' she told him rather sharply. 'It's a payroll for army troops stationed here and to the north, not the contents of a bank vault.

It's in an ironbound chest, I think. About thirty thousand dollars.'

Her eyes were harder now and he wondered if she were changing her mind about him, mistaking his concern for safety and convenience for greed.

'Reckon we'd better scatter,' Dave said, a mite stiffly. 'Make a place to meet again before leaving town.'

'Makes sense,' said Morg, watching the now sober-faced girl.

She hesitated, nodded. 'Yes, it does.'

Dave thought she sounded a little disappointed and smiled to himself. She had had notions of taking over, he figured. Well, maybe she would get her chance later.

* * *

'You should've shot that big black when you had the chance.'

There was a growl in Hank's voice as well as a peevishness as he swigged from the whiskey bottle and handed it across to his drinking companion.

Josh snatched it and took a long draught, coughing a little. 'Mebbe I should've, but it ain't no use cryin' about it now. Wake up, Hank! Wake up and look at the situation *now*! Not yesterday or even an hour ago, or who shoulda done what to which!'

'Hey! Don't spill that whiskey, it's all we got.'

Irritably, Josh slammed the heel of his hand down on the protruding cork and rammed it halfway down the neck. 'And that's all we're havin' for now. We pull this off, we'll buy us a whole damn keg of bonded whiskey . . . mebbe a saloonful.'

'Yeah, *if* we pull it off. I'm startin' to have my doubts, Josh. I mean, we're all takin' it as gospel that Bridget seen Craig hidin' the payroll — *but it ain't certain!* She coulda just said that to stall another whippin'.'

'It's all we got, Hank.' Josh started to his feet, grunting, then started to kick dirt over the small camp-fire which was mostly glowing coals now. 'Come on, let's get to our broncs. You set up in them rocks they call Martha's Chair and I'll move on to the Bird's Nest that overlooks — '

'Huh! You sure picked the cosiest spot!' Hank was surly and buttoned his shirt collar. 'Gettin' chilled-down already an' I ain't even in the wind yet. Hey!! Josh! What the — '

Hank's eyes bulged in the rapidly fading glow of the scattered camp-fire and he clawed at Josh's big hand which was clamped on his throat. He writhed but Josh, bigger, more powerful, *angry*, squeezed harder.

'You ain't showin' the right *attitude*, Hank! Dammit, man! This is our big chance — our *only* chance the way things've been goin' for us lately! You bitch it up, and I swear I'll rip your throat out, and work my way down to your feet, which I'll crush with the biggest rock I can lift!'

He thrust the half-choked man away from him. Hank fell to his knees, holding his throat as he wheezed and

179

coughed while trying to drag in air. He looked up and cringed when he glimpsed Josh's mean face. He felt a boot nudge him roughly in the ribs and he hurriedly got to his feet, staggering. He groped for his six-gun in desperation but there was a whisper of metal sliding out of leather, the ratcheting click of a hammer being cocked, and Hank froze, his bladder suddenly at bursting point.

'J-Jesus, Josh! Wh-what's wrong with you? I ain't done nothin'!' His words were only just distinguishable as he rubbed his aching throat.

'That's the trouble, you been takin' it too damn easy. Now, we're in this together and I expect you to do your part without bitchin'! Savvy?'

Hank nodded, surly, but afraid under it all. Josh was about the meanest ranny he'd ever seen when he felt put out. 'I will, Josh! I will. Swear it on my mother's grave.'

'You could be sharin' it with her, you don't do just like I tell you.'

Hank nodded, trying to keep a blank face.

At least they wouldn't have to share with Kel. Thanks to Josh. Dave Brent's bullet had taken him just above the hip, a mighty painful wound, and Kel wouldn't shut up moaning about it.

So Josh sent Hank to see to the horses and when he got back to camp, Kel was dead. Hank, pale, had looked warily at Josh, who spoke casually as he checked his rifle.

'Pain musta got too much for him. Ticker gave out, I guess . . . '

Hank decided it would be best not to comment.

11

Closing In

Martha's Chair had been named after a schoolgirl. Martha O'Brian had been killed while climbing the precariously stacked rocks. They had given way when she was playing on what — with a little imagination — looked like a giant's chair and Martha had been crushed.

Because most of the piled-up rocks had slipped down, the seat of the chair was now exposed and Hank swore bitterly as he huddled in a worn corduroy jacket against the mountain night wind sweeping in with freezing gusts.

'Damn Josh!' Hank muttered, hugging himself. 'Got himself plenty of shelter in the Bird's Nest. Always picks the best spot for whatever we're doing, whether it's finding a place at a crowded bar or the most weather-proof livery stall for his mount. Just got the knack and the meanness that chokes off other men's protests — if they have any sense.'

He felt tears streaming from his squinted eyes when a chill gust whistled about his head, snatched his hat just in time to save it from blowing off.

By Godfrey! He didn't aim to take much more of this!

Then his thoughts stopped dead and he stood up, now ignoring the wind blasting above the rock he had been sheltering behind.

'Judas *priest*!' he breathed, fumbling for the battered field-glasses down at his side. He got them up to his eyes, muttering as he tried to focus, but couldn't see very clearly in this dim light. If it had been moonlight — but it wasn't. And what's more it really didn't matter, because he could just make out the riders down there as they were silhouetted against the gleaming river, splashed through the shallows, and continued south once across.

Two men and a woman.

He didn't need to be eagle-eyed to figure out who they were!

Subconsciously he touched his still aching throat as he started to clamber down to where his mount was ground-hitched.

For once he'd be taking some good news to Josh Keeler.

* * *

Josh merely grunted when Hank told him what he'd seen, walked to where he had left his horse and swung up into the saddle.

'Let's go,' he said shortly. 'And don't get too close.'

'What if it ain't them?' Hank asked quietly.

He could just make out the expression on Josh's face in the starlight. 'You said it was.'

'Well, I mean, it just about *has* to be, don't it?'

'You better hope so,' Keeler told him flatly. 'Now let's go find out.'

Hank Ivey rubbed his aching throat again as he swallowed audibly and set his horse after the other man.

The wind chilled the sudden sweat on his pinched face. *Josh was heading for one of his mean moods . . .*

★ ★ ★

Case Barlow wasn't looking forward to a long time in the saddle, not the way his rheumatics were playing up. They were giving him hell — he'd noticed a few times before that when he was tense or irritated about something they often seemed to be worse. Or, maybe it was only that he was more active and that drew his attention to them.

He had spent a small fortune with snake-oil salesmen, wanting to believe their outrageous spiels had at least a modicum of truth in the rhetoric. So far he hadn't had a lot of success, but he *did* religiously follow a series of exercises a sawbones in Sweetwater had worked out for his gun arm to keep it as supple as possible.

By hell! He was honest enough to admit to himself that it was only his past legendary prowess with a six-gun that had gotten him out of some tight spots these past few years, but mostly it had been up against Saturday-night drunks.

Case wasn't too damn sure how he would be up against someone who was more than just handy with a six-shooter — and — sober. Like Dave Brent, maybe . . .

There was another worry, too: a few times he had seen Lew Burns eyeing him silently, like he was figuring out whether *he* could outdraw Barlow. If he did, his salary would go through the roof with a success like that under his belt.

And Barlow had enough enemies in Bixby and elsewhere so that there wouldn't be all that much fuss about such an incident: a deputy drawing against his boss, a full-blown sheriff, whose legendary lightning-fast gun arm might be kind of short-circuited these days . . .

But he had been living with these worries for a long time now and knew they had made him bitter and mighty touchy. And he was honest enough with himself to know that his lack of money was really at the base of all these things.

If he could just get together enough to send his wife to one of those specialist doctors in Cheyenne or Denver. She was always nagging him about getting better medical attention: '*It's your fault I'm the way I am!*'

And he had no argument against that . . .

Well, tonight was going to be it, one way or another, he decided, as he looked out his office window to where the mounts and two packhorses were ready and waiting.

He turned quickly, hardly noticing the flashing stab of pain in his hips, as the door opened. He could hear Lew

Burns's gasping breath and the deputy, still looking like hell with all his bruises and cuts, almost shouted, 'They're leavin' town, Case! Headin' south!'

For a moment Case Barlow froze, then he hitched at his gunbelt and said, simply, 'So are we!'

★ ★ ★

Dave and Morg, and probably the girl, were aware they would be watched and followed, but the only way to where the payroll was supposed to be buried was by the southern trail.

Mighty handy for the followers; a damned and dangerous nuisance for those being followed.

There could be lots of twists and turns and backtracking and laying false trails, but the fact remained: there was only the one way to leave the town for a southern destination. It was the geography of the surrounding location that dictated this. Cramped, rising towers of rock forced any traveller towards the river and once that was crossed, there was heavy timber that turned sharply along the base of a sandstone cliff. For years there had been talk about making a tunnel through this cliff, cutting miles off the journey and offering the chance to make trails towards other points of the compass, but nothing had yet been done. This was all general knowledge to the locals, and strangers heeded it because it made sense the way the country was laid out.

But certain local folk over the years had found old Indian trails that could take a rider over the sandstone cliff and safely down the other side, saving miles.

Bridget knew of two of these trails. Her father, Old Hans Gerholdt, had known and used them for distributing the rotgut redeye he brewed in the tangled hills behind their small ranch outside of Bixby. The girl had helped him many a time to drive mules laden with kegs and bottles of the fiery booze over these hidden trails.

Now she led Morg and Dave with

confidence up a steep, narrow path that clung to the cliffs like a twisted string wrapped around a pudding, wide enough for two riders side by side in places; at others it seemed that even a lizard would think twice about continuing.

Dave was a man who was leery of heights, though he had never had a real hang-up about them, but he was always glad when he had negotiated high trails successfully. This one made him cringe, and Morg, too, seemed hesitant, but would not show any reluctance (and *definitely* no fear!) in front of Bridget. Dave merely sweated his way in silence.

Once he paused to look back to check if anyone was following, and both times his mouth went so dry his tongue stuck to the roof. Morg noticed and grinned with the recklessness of youth and boundless energy.

The girl said nothing. He didn't even hear her breathing hard and she seemed to have her mount trained to simply follow where she indicated.

The black was uneasy and Dave was surprised when Bridget edged back, soothed the horse with easy talk and strokings.

'I can lead him if you want,' she offered.

Dave hesitated, then shook his head. 'Obliged, Bridget, but, no, he's mine and he'll have to get used to going where I want to go, whether he likes it or not.'

Even in the starlight, fading now the moon was starting to rise over the hills, he saw her eyes glint and narrow slightly.

'He won't react well to rough discipline,' she said in clipped, disapproving tones.

'He's never had rough discipline,' Dave answered curtly, a mite peeved. 'I don't treat my animals that way.'

Her teeth flashed briefly. 'I already guessed that. I took a good look at your black before we left: he's in fine, unmarked condition.'

Curious, Dave asked, 'And if he'd

showed signs of taking a hard cuff or two?'

'I would've asked how he came by them and — depending on your answer — either would've smiled or shot you.'

Dave blinked. *Jesus!* he thought. *A little thing like this girl not backing off an inch!* 'Your father teach you that?'

'Yes. People saw him only as an old drunk, didn't know him in his younger years. He came from a well-off family that bred horses for show and — ' She stopped, shrugged. 'There was some trouble with one of his clients. I don't know the details, but he had to leave his family and ended up here where . . . well, you don't need to know the rest.'

'I'd be interested, though.'

'Perhaps, some time. Hey, Morgan! The next bend is very sharp. Take extra care.' *A bit bossy!* Dave thought.

'Whatever you say, Bridget. How about comin' up and keepin' me company?'

She laughed. 'Why not?'

She flashed Dave a smile and moved on ahead to edge up beside the tall youngster.

He smiled at the sight, Morg's long, slim form, bending down almost double to slip an arm about the small girl's shoulders and plant a kiss on her cheek.

Some time and place for romance, he thought, then sobered as, looking back and down, just as the moon's orb spread pale light over the slopes, he saw — and heard — another horse and the man with it, fighting it while holding the bit.

'Someone's following!' he called softly and heard Morg curse, which earned him a light slap from Bridget.

'We'll lose them on the way down the other side,' she called back softly. 'Don't worry, Dave. I know these hills well.'

Hell! he thought. *This slip of a girl* — again! — trying to make *him* feel easier! And him standing still for it. He must be getting old.

★ ★ ★

Josh Keeler and Hank Ivey had reached the edge of the Big Salty early in the evening and had set up their camp at the place Josh had called the Bird's Nest.

As the name implied, it was high up the face of the steep side of the mountain and afforded a good view of the salt flats, or would do so when the sun came up.

The Big Salty showed as a slightly glowing lighter patch that stretched almost to the horizon, the moonlight reflecting enough to make a man squint if he looked that way for too long.

They had taken turns at lookout and now Hank came back from his observation point, rubbing his hands briskly together.

'Gettin' cold up here, Josh.'

'Then huddle down, but don't light no fires.'

'Didn't aim to, but someone did.'

Josh snapped his head up as he lit a cigarette.

'Did what?'

'Light a fire. Down in that hollow near the edge of the salt.'

'Christ, the man's mad, whoever he is.'

'No, Josh, I think he knows what he's doin'. Didn't let it get any bigger than he wanted and it won't show from down there. Just that bein' a bit higher here, we can see it.' By now Josh was stretched out on the edge of the trail with the field-glasses up to his eyes.

'Ain't worth spit in this light!' Josh growled, shaking the glasses as if that would make them show an image better. 'We best go down and take a look.'

'Aw, *hell*, Josh! I been on lookout for hours — I'm dead.'

'Could be closer than you think . . . we go down.'

So they went down, leaving the horses and taking care to move without making too much noise. They dropped about twenty feet down the narrow strip of trail, to a small camp, studying the lumpy bedroll with a hat at the top, between a boulder and the small fire, the occupant no doubt enjoying the reflected heat and sleeping easy.

Using signs, Josh waved Hank around so that they would approach from both ends of the bedroll. They were on hands and knees, guns out, closing in, when a voice spoke behind them. 'You fellers lose somethin'?'

Both Josh and Hank rolled swiftly onto their backs, lifting their guns. But they didn't fire. A tall man was standing beside the boulder, hatless, holding a shotgun pointed at them. His face was lined with fatigue, eyes hard.

'Drop the Colts — or leather 'em, if you do it careful.' As he spoke, he cocked the Greener's hammers and Josh and Hank put their guns away, very carefully. The man made them sit, knees raised, hands locked together by intertwined fingers beneath their thighs.

'That looks good,' he commented. He sounded fairly young and when he turned a little they saw he was around his mid-twenties. He stomped his feet.

'A whole damn lot colder up here than where I come from! You fellers got names?'

'Why you want to know?' Josh asked.

'Your *names*!' the shotgunner snapped, jerking the gun, and they mumbled them.

'Didn't quite make 'em out, gents, but they didn't sound like the one I wanted to hear.'

'Which one's that?' Hank spoke up.

The man hesitated briefly. 'Dave Brent — know him?'

Josh said quickly, 'Could be a name we've heard. Friend of yours?'

'Not that you'd notice! He killed two of my brothers and a third one I was travellin' up here with rode off a cliff in the dark. My old man was stomped to death by a hoss he was breakin' in to come lookin' for Brent. One way or another, you might say the son of a bitch wiped out my whole damn family!'

'Judas! You're ridin' under a bad-luck star, mister!' commented Hank. 'You got a name, or shouldn't I ask?'

'It likely won't mean anything to you, but I'm Pierce Vandemann and I've come a thousand miles to find this Brent.'

'I knew a Vandemann down on the border long time ago.' Josh looked thoughtful. 'Big Will?'

'That was my old man.' In a slower voice, he said, 'I'm the only Vandemann left now and I . . . well, I gotta kill this goddamn Brent before the sonuver kills me and wipes the Vandemanns off the face of the earth.'

'Feel like a cup of coffee?' Josh asked in friendly tones. 'We might be able to help you out . . . '

12

The Spoils

This part of the country was seeing more activity than it had known for years.

The railroad was operating regularly, though its schedules had been reduced after initially carrying building supplies to the new towns and ranches that were establishing themselves in various places selected by new settlers. Hopefully, more freight would be carried as other pioneers settled and the holdings expanded and more building materials, even stock, would be needed.

This kind of temporary suspension of activity was helpful for the groups that were gathering in the area — attracted by stories of the lost railroad payroll. But while all knew what they were searching for, they didn't necessarily know where to search.

Not all of them, anyway.

Josh was aware of this and set up two men, Clancy and Donner, on a scrubby ridge that gave them a wider and longer view of where he figured the others would be searching.

'You spot 'em anywhere near that zone I showed you let me know *pronto*! The moment you see *anyone* in that area, you get a signal off — I'll see it.' He saw the worry on their faces at his tone and made himself smile, although there wasn't a deal of warmth in it. 'Bonus to the man who gets first signal to me. All right?'

That went down with the others well enough, and Josh felt confident he would know before anyone else who was searching — and where.

At the same time, Bridget was content to have Dave and Morg with her and just hoped she could recollect the landmarks. It was an empty part of the world here, not much vegetation, which meant fewer animals, so it was also quieter, eerie — a few birds calling, the occasional cough or snort or a dying scream as some predator hunted in the sparse brush.

These things — and lack of the normal cacophony of the denizens of a more vegetated area — gave the place a touch of mystery, perhaps even of menace.

If that was a slight exaggeration, the search teams all had similar thoughts — if expressed differently — and went carefully about their business.

Dave and Morg had followed Bridget and she had seemed to take one hell of a long time to get where she was going. Or, maybe it *wasn't* where she wanted to go . . .

Dave put the big black up alongside her roan. 'We finally there?'

The girl looked at him quickly and a slow smile moved her full lips. 'Impatient to be rich?'

'Just impatient,' Dave admitted quietly. 'We've passed that needle rock twice and I figure we crossed the river at least three times.'

She continued to look at him with that enigmatic smile. 'Those bends can be confusing, but — look around you.'

Frowning, and becoming annoyed when he saw Morg Longstreet watching with a kind of smirk, Dave said, 'All I see is scattered brush, a couple of scrawny trees and, beyond, too much damn salt and not enough water.'

'But no other riders,' she pointed out and quickly lifted a small hand off the saddlehorn. 'They could be under cover, yes, but I'm pretty sure I've bamboozled anyone hoping that I'd lead them to the payroll area.'

'Including me.'

'Good! Now if we wait a little longer the moon'll clear the hills and we'll be able to see the landmarks I'm looking for.'

Morg sniggered and finally Dave smiled crookedly.

'OK, OK! I've had my turn at bitching *and* out of place, too, so — '
He swept off his battered hat and

executed a cramped, but mostly adequate bow in his saddle. 'I've usually been the teacher, rather than the pupil. Carry on, ma'am: where you lead, I'll follow.'

Morg laughed shortly. 'Got you that time, didn't she?'

'I'll remember,' Dave replied with a growl which he quickly tempered with a twisted smile.

Bridget laughed, and he liked the sound: it was genuine, unaffected amusement.

Morg asked, 'How long we gotta wait, Bridge?' He gestured to where the crest of a large salt dune was starting to outline. 'That moon's waxin' and it'll be mighty bright.'

'Yes, we should get going,' she said, standing in her stirrups and looking around at the countryside that was beginning to show more clearly by the minute. She pointed. 'There's the first landmark.'

Both Dave and Morg looked in the direction she was pointing, but they shook their heads. 'All I see is a lot more dunes,' Morg allowed, and Dave grunted agreement.

'That's it. Move this way a little — not too far! — just come up on my left. Now d'you see anything unusual?'

'Only that you got three dead bugs in the crown of your hat,' Morg said, and laughed as she took a swipe at him. Dave thought he was lucky it didn't land: it might've knocked him out of the saddle.

'*Look, you blind idiot! Look!* Between that first and second row of sandhills. They run almost straight, and at the end of the row, where they start to curve, what do you see?'

'Nothin' much — only a bright star . . . ?'

'Which star?' she asked in exasperation.

'The North Star,' Dave said quietly, and felt a slight tingle of rising excitement.

'*Yes!* The North Star. And what's beneath it?'

'*Beneath?* Judas, Bridge, you could ride till doomsday and not be under the damn star!'

'I know *that*!' she said sharply. 'But what appears to be beneath that star from this position?'

Morg stood in his stirrups, his height giving him an advantage over the short girl. Dave lifted up, too, and saw what looked like a pool of deep shadow, almost like the silhouette of a giant . . . tooth.

'What's makin' that shadow?' he asked, and the girl smiled.

'At least someone's got good eyesight!'

'Hey! I see it, too! What is it, Bridget? I don't see any rocks that'd throw that kinda shad — *Wait!*' *Damn!* I moved my head a bit and — It's the crests of the dunes, ain't it? Two, three rows of 'em almost in line, but not quite. The curve on one dune half-blocks the one on the next and so on. Makes it look all ragged! Kinda . . . sawtoothed.'

'That's right,' the girl said. 'Even in

daylight if you get the line-up just right — and you can do that only from this place where we are now — it still looks like a giant broken tooth.'

'So?' Morg asked impatiently.

'And right at the bottom of that 'tooth' is a scattering of boulders. Under one of them — and I know which one — is where Craig buried the payroll chest.'

Both men glanced at each other and Dave swung his gaze to the girl, noticed her face looked slightly grey in the reflected light, her mouth in a tight line.

'What else is buried there?' he asked quietly and she lifted her eyes towards his face.

'The guards, of course. Craig shot them so callously. Virtually just . . . kicked them into the hole.'

'Well, dead men wouldn't've spent much even if they got the chest open!' quipped Morg, but raised only a half-smile from Dave and none at all from the girl.

'They were ordinary men, Morg,'

Dave pointed out quietly. 'Died just because they were working at their jobs guarding the payroll.'

'Murdered in cold blood,' she said heavily. 'They've had no real burial, not even the decency of a blanket wrapped around them. Craig just dumped them in the hole. Threw a few spadefuls of sand on top and pushed a boulder into place.' She may have given a slight shudder as she finished.

'I'll open the grave,' Dave offered quietly.

Bridget glanced at him quickly. 'All right. Yes, you might as well make your contribution. What'll yours be, Morg?'

Morg ran a tongue around his lips. 'I guess I can give Dave a hand.'

'Then let's not waste any more time: we don't want to lose the moonlight. Rising like that, it's changing the dunes' shadows all the time, too.'

'Let's go get the spoils,' Dave said.

It was far from being a pleasant job.

The girl stood well back at first but somehow steeled herself and got down on hands and knees, dragged armfuls of sand aside. But when the first clawed hand appeared, poking up, *pointing in her direction, it seemed*, she bounded up and hurried off several yards, hacking and hawking.

There was little smell but it was still far from pleasant and Dave and Morg tied bandannas around their faces. Bridget stood well back and when the men spread out one of Dave's worn blankets, she started to pull up some brush. She didn't watch as they exhumed the murdered guards and wrapped them in the blanket, but, holding a kerchief to her lower face, she indicated where she had cleared the brush and the men moved the corpses across. Morg made the depressions left by the torn-up bushes a little longer and deeper.

Bridget looked a little queasy and Dave took pity on her, turned her away and gave her a light push. Then he and Morg covered the blanket and its contents with the bushes and scooped some sand into the depression.

Looking down into the hole they had dug under the boulders, they saw the iron-bound edge of a chest poking out through loose sand that had trickled back after the dead men had been removed.

'My God! It's — it's still here!' she gasped.

'Thought you knew that all along,' Dave commented, and she shrugged.

'Yes, I saw it buried, but I-I don't know. I thought there might be some bad luck attached to it, the way those guards were so coldly murdered, and someone may've found it.' She seemed uneasy, and added, 'I didn't think anything good could come of such a thing.' She paused and smiled, lifting her arms out from her sides. 'Silly superstition, I suppose.'

'Well, it's a three-way split now, Bridget,' Morg Longstreet said cheerfully.

A slight frown appeared on her face and she moved her gaze to Dave, who kept his face deadpan.

'Does that sound fair to you, Dave?' she asked quietly.

'Of course it's fair!' Morg cut in a little curtly. 'We're all three here, ain't we? We found it together. I mean, we all did our own little bits and . . . here it is. Three of us found it, we split it three ways. Can't get fairer than that.'

'Sounds fair,' Dave agreed, and the girl nodded slowly. 'Except it's not our money, Morg. Belongs to the army.'

'And they lost it because they didn't take proper care of it!' Morg said, showing his rising irritability now. 'Ever heard of finders keepers, Dave?'

'Morg — ' the girl started but, frowning, he made a sharp gesture with his hands, cutting off her words.

'Hold on, Bridget — Dave?'

'We keep it, it's just like we're stealing it from the army, Morg, when we know it belongs to them.'

Morg made an impatient gesture and there was a lot of anger in the movement and his rising voice.

'You didn't seem to think it was such a bad idea when I first mentioned we look for it and share!'

'No, but we said we could mebbe just claim a reward for finding it.'

'Hell! Who knows how much that'd be! It's not a helluva big payroll! What would they offer? Five per cent? Even ten wouldn't amount to much.'

'It'd be honest money.'

'Judas priest!' Morg threw his arms in the air briefly. 'Come *on*, Dave! Look, the men that money was meant for have been paid long ago. The army's writ this off as lost! We were lucky enough to find it so it's *ours*! That's the way I see it!'

Dave just shook his head — once. 'Wrong, Morg.'

'Well, what makes you so damn holy about it?'

'Morg!' the girl said sharply and when he looked at her she said, just as tartly, 'Dave is just trying to do the right thing.'

'Aw, I give up! Look, the damn army

— and there ain't a truly poor one anywhere! — has give up on this, put it in their books as a loss. Now, that's their bad luck. They coulda found it if they'd looked harder, but we found it, so it's ours! Christ, can't you see that?'

Dave surprised him by nodding gently. 'Yeah, I see it, Morg. It's good enough reasoning, but don't take any moral side into account.'

'Well, you see how many drinks and plates of grub you can buy with morals!'

'Morg, when you get right down to it, Bridget's the one who found it; we just did the rough work for her.'

Morg looked at the girl sharply. 'Well, yeah, I guess that's right. You ain't said much, Bridget. You for us keepin' it or turnin' it in for a reward?'

'Don't really matter what she thinks, does it?'

They all swung quickly towards the harsh voice that spoke from the edge of the brush.

Three men with guns stood there: the

barrels jerked upwards. 'Get 'em up!'

Slowly, Dave and Morg lifted their hands. The girl stood very still.

Josh Keeler smiled crookedly at Dave. 'Thanks for doin' all the hard work.' He gestured towards the excavation.

'Left just enough room to squeeze you in, Josh.'

Josh made a snorting sound, looked around at Hank and Pierce Vandemann. 'Don't scare easy, do he?'

Hank curled a lip. Pierce pushed his hat back and took a step forward. 'Mebbe that's because he ain't recognized me yet.'

'I see you, Pierce. Bring the rest of the clan?'

'You son of a bitch! *I'm* all there's left of the Vandemanns! Ha! Surprised, huh?'

'I am,' Dave admitted slowly. 'What happened?'

'*You* happened, you bastard!'

'I haven't been near any of you miserable Vandemanns for nigh on a year. The hell're you talkin' about?'

'You'll find out an' what I got waitin' for you'll make you wish you'd never been born!'

13

What Money?

Josh had Donner and Clancy with him, as well as Hank Ivey and Pierce Vandemann.

All were armed and by the looks on their faces, wouldn't lose a minute's sleep over pulling their triggers on Josh Keeler's say-so.

Dave wondered just how long that would be coming.

Then he said, 'You've got nothing against the girl, Josh. She just sort of got dragged into this.'

Josh cupped his left hand around his ear, leaning slightly forward. 'Huh? What was that . . . ? *Let her go*, you mean? Hmm. Well, I'd *like* to — you know that, don't you, Bridget — dear wife of mine?'

'Oh, sure, Josh, you're so fair-minded

and compassionate!'

Josh grinned. 'Feisty, ain't she? Dave, look — I let her go, what you think'll happen? She'll go back an' carry on with her life as usual? Mebbe I oughta give her a share and that'd hold her . . . ?' He shook his head vigorously. 'Naaaah! You know damn well what she'd do! Go straight to that old has-been Case Barlow and tell him everythin'.' His face hardened abruptly, as he walked up to Dave and rammed the muzzle of his rifle hard into his midriff.

Dave's breath gusted as he grabbed at his stomach, knees giving way. He stumbled as he fell and Josh's boots were waiting. He kicked Dave hard, twice, once in the chest, the other in the side. Dave just managed to partially protect his ribs with his left arm.

Pain engulfed him and his head rang with a cacophony of sound, but he heard Josh Keeler's cold voice say, 'Just keep your stupid suggestions to yourself from now on, Dave, or I'll do some dental work on you — with my boots!'

Dave grunted, and another kick jarred his upper chest to emphasize Josh's threat.

'Leave him alone!' the girl shouted and even took a step towards Josh who, after looking initially surprised, now grinned bleakly.

'Mebbe I'll start on you.'

She surprised everyone by smiling. 'Oh, I'd like that!'

Frowning, he said, 'We've had some fun in the past, honey, but this time I don't think so!'

Her hand moved under her vest and when it appeared again, she was holding a short-bladed knife that gleamed in the moonlight. 'You sure?'

He didn't like looking at the knife, that was obvious. Dave wondered how many times she had threatened him with it previously . . . or maybe used it?

'You know we were never even married, Josh. My father wasn't a preacher.'

'Hell, who cares?' Josh laughed. 'An'

toss that toothpick away before I have Hank take it off you.'

The other two men, Donner and Clancy — both work-hardened cowpokes who did whatever Josh required of them, simply because he paid well — stood there, unsmiling, holding their guns. Waiting.

Like a pair of vultures impatient for the feasting to begin.

Dave could see that the girl was mighty leery of them. She hesitated just a moment longer, then let the knife fall. Josh swung his gaze to Dave.

'Don't think I'll worry about you, Dave.' He nodded again, this time in the direction of Pierce Vandemann. 'Reckon Pierce there has some plans of his own for you.'

'You can say that again!' agreed Pierce, his face taut and bleak as he regarded the man he considered was responsible for the loss of all his family.

Dave said nothing, merely looked at the hostile Vandemann and shook his head once.

Pierce smiled. It was totally devoid of even a suggestion of mirth.

Dave was perplexed: how could Pierce blame him for wiping out his family? But he had more pressing things to worry about right now.

'Dave,' Josh said suddenly. 'You ain't gonna gimme an argument about that payroll, are you?'

'Well, not right now.'

Josh grinned. 'Good enough. So, now it's only a matter of what we do with you and the little bitch there.'

'You're forgetting Morg,' Dave pointed out.

'Aw, no, I'm not. He's been a pain in my butt for a long, long time. Know just what I'm gonna do with him.'

The girl gave a small cry and Dave jumped as Josh casually swung his Colt around and triggered. Morg's head snapped back as the bullet knocked him clear off his feet. He rolled once, flopped onto his bloody face in the sand.

'You — you murdering swine!'

Bridget choked and launched herself at Josh but Donner, the bigger of the two hardcases, stepped in front of her and placed a large hand against her chest. Without straining he pushed and she flew backwards and fell to the ground. Clancy, a man who seemed to have a crooked smile permanently in place, waved his gun in front of Dave as he started forward to help the girl.

'Forget about bein' a gennleman,' Clancy grated.

Dave stopped in his tracks and by then the dazed girl was struggling to her feet. Dave's eyes met Josh's.

'She was too polite, Josh, I can think of something much worse to call you.'

Josh laughed. 'You know you're beat, Dave, and it's about your turn to leave us.' He raised his Colt and Dave froze. Josh looked at him coldly. 'No, not yet. I think I'll mebbe let Pierce there think up something very special for you.'

'Way ahead of you, Josh,' Pierce said. 'But I can wait. Like to think about it, picture how good ol' Dave is gonna writhe and moan while he's dyin'. See how right I am.'

'Like your thinkin', Pierce. How about you, Dave? You like what's waitin' for you?'

'Not especially, but I like what's waiting for *you*, Josh.'

Josh's grin tightened a little and he hit Dave in the side, just where he'd kicked him in the ribs. Dave moaned and doubled up, took a knee against his forehead that sent him reeling back, arms flailing. He went down and, as Josh moved in swiftly with right boot raised, Bridget stepped between the downed man and Josh.

She spat in his face.

The world seemed to hang suspended, nothing moving, nothing making a sound.

Then Josh roared, clawed a hand down his face and lunged at the girl. She dodged quickly and Dave made his move, rising to drive a fist against Josh's jaw. The blow sent the man reeling. Pierce instinctively jumped out of the way. Dave was like a wild man, arms flailing, pushing, striking, smashing his fists into the dazed Josh's face.

The man went down to one knee and Dave managed to lift his own right knee into that bloody face before Donner picked him up bodily, grunted a little, and threw him five yards, spinning through the air.

Dave landed all asprawl and instinctively used the impetus of the fall to keep rolling — away from Donner. Clancy came in from the other side, though, gun in one hand, the barrel trying to follow Dave's fast ducking and dodging.

He fired and the bullet missed Dave and *zzziipped!* into the sand.

Pierce Vandemann yelled, 'Don't kill him! Not yet!'

Dave, half on his feet, twisted painfully and launched himself headlong in Pierce's direction. Vandemann was caught unawares and, though he raised his gun swiftly and took a swipe at Dave's head, he missed and stumbled to his knees.

Dave kicked him in the head and yanked the pistol from his grasp. Unsteady on his feet, he spun and triggered. Donner stopped in his tracks, blinked and looked down at a hole in his chest spurting blood. Still looking surprised he raised his own gun, hand shaking.

Dave shot him again and the big man sighed, thumped to his knees, then, making what sounded like a long yawn, fell face down and was still.

By that time, Dave was on the move, leaping over Clancy, who had dived for the ground, swinging the gun back-handed in time to catch Josh a glancing blow on the side of the head. The man dropped to hands and knees but wasn't knocked out cold. He stayed kneeling, hanging his head and moaning.

Pierce Vandemann was shouting, yet staying clear of the violence. But now he saw Dave running to help the girl, went into a crouch and held his other six-gun in both hands, trying to line up the blade foresight on Dave Brent's constantly moving form.

Then Morg, blood trickling down from his hairline, suddenly pushed up, groggily, and kicked Pierce in the left knee. The man yelled in agony as he fell, twisting, gun firing wild.

Hank had run to the outskirts of the drama and was lining up his gun on Dave, who had paused, crouching, as he swiftly checked cartridges in the Colt's cylinder.

'Dave! Look out!' screamed Bridget and Dave simply hurled himself headlong, heard a Colt hammer three fast shots and got sand kicked into his face.

He spun half onto his back, saw Clancy was the shooter, and chopped at the hammer spur with the edge of his left hand. He put his last two bullets into Clancy's big chest. The impact knocked the man sideways and down — where he stayed.

The moment Dave fired, he threw himself to one side and floundered down a short slope.

Sand and dust kicked up by all the action and wild movement of the people, together with the clouds of gunsmoke, made things mighty hazy. But even as he rolled, Dave checked the Colt's cylinder, swore when he saw only empty chambers.

His own Colt was still in his holster and he dropped the empty one, and rather than try to shuck loads from his belt and thumb them home into the cylinder, he drew his own weapon. *Fast!* He ducked as a couple of stray bullets struck sparks from the metal-bound money chest and ricocheted away with hornet whines.

A shadow fell across him and he looked up sharply. Pierce Vandemann towered above him, face smeared with black powder and grime, sand even clinging to the sweat on his skin.

'You're a goddamn one-man army, Brent! But you ain't gonna deprive me of my revenge!'

Dave started to lunge forward, still holding his gun by the middle, with the butt away from him, as Pierce levelled his Colt at Dave's head.

'*Hold it! Right now!*' roared a voice. 'Judas priest, there's been enough killin'! You drop that gun, feller, or I'll blow your head off your shoulders!'

Sheriff Case Barlow, with Deputy Burns beside him, holding a sawn-off shotgun, stood on the rise, menacing the group below him. 'Leather that damn gun, Brent!'

Dave pushed his gun back into his holster and swung his left fist against Pierce Vandemann's jaw.

Pierce staggered and swayed off balance, and Barlow shouted at Dave, 'By God! You take some chances!'

Dave lifted his hands shoulder-high. 'Good to see you again, Sheriff.'

'You may not think so shortly!'

The two lawmen came down the slope carefully, Barlow first, stumbling with his rheumatics, while Burns covered the rest, shotgun cocked.

'You got some nice moves, Brent,' Burns said grudgingly.

Dave glanced at him, then at the dazed Pierce Vandemann, the man's eyes starting to focus on him like gun muzzles. 'Christ! You're a hard man to kill!' Pierce rasped.

'No, he ain't!'

Dave jerked his head up, saw Josh Keeler's contorted face as the man lifted his gun . . . and Dave was looking right down the barrel.

He spun away, right hand blurring down and up, shooting twice, the barrel slanted slightly upwards.

The bullets took Josh low down and actually lifted him off the ground. He crashed onto his back, his boots kicking and scrabbling at the sand for most of a minute before they were still.

By that time the dishevelled Dave was swaying on his feet. The dazed, scalp-creased Morg was being steadied by the girl, but Pierce Vandemann still held his gun on Dave.

'*Judas priest!*' he breathed. 'Josh was right! You damned well *are* a hard man to kill! But I'm here to do it and I aim to — '

'You deaf?' shouted Case Barlow.

'You think I won't shoot?'

Pierce froze, glanced at Barlow's determined face and lifted his hands slowly. 'He's a murderer, Sheriff! Killed my whole damn family!' His voice broke on the last word.

'Ah, shove it, Pierce!' Dave's voice was harsh with fatigue and sounded as if he didn't care a damn from this moment on — then reached out and snatched the gun from Pierce's hand. He swiftly reversed his hold and Vandemann stiffened, face drawn and frozen into apprehensive lines, knowing he was only seconds from dying . . .

'You shoot an' you're dead, Brent!'

Dave looked at Barlow and saw the man meant it.

He dropped the gun. 'OK, but he's loco! I haven't been near any of his family for nigh on a year.'

'That right, boy?' Barlow snapped and Pierce nodded jerkily.

'That don't mean he didn't — '

'Ah, relax, you damn fool!' Dave sounded disgusted. 'So you're the last of the Vandemanns, well, I guess even that's a good enough reason to let you live. But, you just get one thing straight, Pierce — and get it *damned* straight! — I never wiped out your family. Yeah, I shot them two young brothers in that gunfight, but even that was unavoidable. I mean, they were shootin' at me and I shot back, didn't know who they were or even care. Just wanted to stop 'em killing me.'

Pierce glared. 'You — you put a hex on our family! Even Pa breakin' in a hoss to come lookin' for you, he — The damn hoss stomped him to death!'

Dave waited a moment. 'You can't blame *that* on me, for Chris'sakes, Pierce!'

'Do sound kinda mixed-up, son,' the sheriff allowed, frowning, still looking hard at Dave. *The way Dave'd gotten his gun out to nail Josh! Hell almighty! It was as fast — mebbe faster — than his own draw!*

Millie could be right: it was a good time for him to consider retirement whether they could afford it or not.

Pierce seemed to have some trouble with his eyes, brushed at them with a hand and took a deep breath. His voice was kind of strangled when he spoke. 'All right. All *right*! It sounds stupid, maybe, but the fact remains, I've lost my whole family, and most of it was linked to you some way or t'other, Brent!'

'Well, unlink it, Pierce! Dammit, boy, I hardly recall how it all started. You Vandemanns were trying to kill me — two of you! I shot 'em both and — well, I guess that was it. Now tell me, was I s'posed to stand still while they shot me? That's how your old man figured!'

Pierce licked his lips. 'Aw, Pa was all right. Not too brainy, mebbe, but he was an all right father, good to Ma. Yeah, well . . . Look, I gotta do some thinkin' on this, Dave. It all kinda makes me sick.' His voice cracked as he added, 'I'm the last Vandemann. I gotta do somethin' to square things.'

Dave waited a few moments, then

said, quietly, 'You're startin' to sound reasonable, Pierce. Too early to think about shakin' hands, I guess?'

'Damn right it is!' snapped Pierce and turned swiftly and walked away.

Dave thought his hunched shoulders might have been shaking a little as he walked, head down. A decent enough man at heart. Dave hoped he would come around — and soon.

He jumped when someone took his arm and Bridget smiled up at him. 'I think you're a good man, Dave Brent.'

He arched his eyebrows. 'An' I think you're a fine-lookin' woman, but where does that get us?'

Her grip tightened on his arm. 'Why don't we wait and see?'

He smiled. 'Why don't we?'

'Aw, now, don't that kinda tug at your heart strings, Lew?' Sheriff Barlow said, and the deputy shrugged.

'I take back what I said, Sheriff,' Dave said coldly. 'It *ain't* so good to see you.'

Barlow even smiled at that. 'Told you

you'd feel that way. There'll be no more killin'! And that payroll goes straight back to where it belongs!' He looked around, eyes bleak. 'Anyone want to give me an argument on that?'

No one did.

'And you still broke outa my jail — not to mention, assaulted good ol' Lew there.'

'Hell, you know I shouldn't've been in jail in the first place!' Dave said harshly. He turned to face Barlow squarely, right hand crooking a little as he let it hang down at his side, putting it on a level with his gun butt.

'Aw now, boy, you ain't loco enough to try and outdraw *me*, are you?'

Dave froze: he hadn't consciously prepared for a shoot-out; he lifted both hands out from his sides. 'I guess I just reacted, Case.'

'You damn near got yourself killed!' cut in Lew Burns. 'Tryin' to outdraw Case Barlow, for Chris'sakes!'

He made a disparaging sound and shook his head in disbelief that anyone would be so loco.

But Dave watched Barlow's old face and — *just for a fleeting moment* — he saw a shade of doubt in the man's eyes. They made contact with Dave's as he just let his arms drop to his sides, relaxed.

'Must've had a mad moment, Case.'

The lawman seemed to be thinking of something else — and he was. If Burns's wife kept nagging at him to give up the deputy's job, well, Dave Brent could easily fill the bill. Barlow figured the man wouldn't mind a job here in Bixby where he could be close to Bridget.

He realized they were all looking at him and he cleared his throat, nodded jerkily. 'Lucky you come to your senses in time. We'll talk about your escape when we — ' His voice was rough and he looked away. 'I think Morg's tryin' to get our attention.'

Dave thought it was Barlow's way of changing the subject, a little shaky, as the old gunfighter realized he hadn't been so sure of his own gunspeed.

But then Morg Longstreet called them across to where he was squatting beside the strongbox, head bound with a strip torn from the girl's skirt. The lid of the chest was open. 'Hey! Come look at this.'

'How'd you get that open?' Dave asked as they approached the group gathered around the strongbox.

'Ricochet durin' the fight — busted the lock. But looky here — at the 'money'.'

'What money?' Sheriff Barlow growled, staring down at a mixture of gravel and a couple of handfuls of old and rusting nuts and bolts.

'I don't understand,' said the girl.

Morg grinned, swayed a little but steadied and held up a crumpled and filthy piece of paper. 'This was stuffed into that mess in there.'

They smoothed it, read it, though the words were barely legible.

This is for you, you thieving swine. Yes, that's what you are if you're reading this! this chest of rubbish was specially prepared for you, whoever you are.

In case you are too dumb to work it out, This strongbox was a decoy in case fools like you had notions of stealing the army payroll, which arrived safely two weeks ago by another train.

Hard luck for you!

We wish you much, much, more of the same!

Sincerely

Wyoming and Colorado Railroad Company

Dave looked at the girl and the wounded Morg, then at the lawmen and, finally, at the dead men strewn around.

There didn't seem to be anything to say.

We do hope that you have enjoyed reading this large print book.

Did you know that all of our titles are available for purchase?

We publish a wide range of high quality large print books including:
Romances, Mysteries, Classics
General Fiction
Non Fiction and Westerns

Special interest titles available in large print are:
The Little Oxford Dictionary
Music Book, Song Book
Hymn Book, Service Book

Also available from us courtesy of Oxford University Press:
Young Readers' Dictionary
(large print edition)
Young Readers' Thesaurus
(large print edition)

For further information or a free brochure, please contact us at:
Ulverscroft Large Print Books Ltd.,
The Green, Bradgate Road, Anstey,
Leicester, LE7 7FU, England.
Tel: (00 44) **0116 236 4325**
Fax: (00 44) **0116 234 0205**

TWO GUNS NORTH

Neil Hunter

Jason Brand's latest assignment takes him into the mountains, searching for two missing men — a Deputy US Marshal and a government geologist. But this apparently routine assignment turns out to be anything but. For Bodie the Stalker, hunting a brutal killer, rides the same trail. It's just another manhunt for him — until he finds himself on the wrong end of the chase. But then Bodie meets Brand. And when they join forces, it's as if Hell itself has come to the high country . . .

GUNS OF THE BRASADA

Neil Hunter

Ballard and McCall are in Texas, working for Henry Conway, an old friend, on the Lazy-C ranch. But trouble is brewing: Yancey Merrick, owner of the big Diamond-M, kept pushing to expand his empire. Then Henry's son Harry is run down through the brasada thicket before being shot in the back and killed. Determined to find the guilty party, Ballard and McCall suddenly find themselves deep in a developing range war . . .

LONELY RIDER

Steve Hayes

He calls himself 'Melody', after the word burned inside his belt. Because he can't remember his own name — or anything at all prior to the past six weeks. It's 'amnesia', according to Regan Avery, the woman he rescues from a fast-flowing river. But Melody doesn't need the fancy name for his predicament to know he's in trouble — for the few things he *can* remember involve being shot at and wounded, with a posse hard on his heels . . .

GILA MONSTER

Colin Bainbridge

A stagecoach is on its way to the small town of Medicine Bend when it is attacked by outlaws. However, the coach's passengers manage to repel them. This disparate array of characters — the new marshal Wade Calvin; Mr Taber, insurance salesman; and Miss Jowett, on her way to take on caring for her widowed nephew's children — thus find their lives intertwined. But as they settle into life in Medicine Bend, Gila Goad, the outlaws' vicious leader, hears news of the botched robbery — and is determined to get his revenge . . .

THE GUN MASTER

Rory Black

On his way to visit an old friend, Rex Carey arrives in the township of Willow Creek. But, unbeknownst to him, the infamous Zane Black is staying in the same hotel. Soon Rex, known throughout the West as the Gun Master, clashes with Zane, and blood is spilled. Meanwhile, Forrest Black is riding towards Willow Creek with his men, with no idea he is about to find his brother Zane dead. Determined to avenge him, Forrest and his outlaw gang are on a collision course with Rex . . .

SHOT TO HELL

Scott Connor

Bounty hunter Jarrett Wade gained his fierce reputation when he defeated the bandit Orlando Pyle in Hamilton. But, several years on, Wade has lost his edge, and is reduced to taking any lowly assignment he can find. A chance to regain his past glory appears when he's offered an apparently simple assignment. He readily accepts — but before he can complete the task, he's gunned down and left for dead . . .